The Ally

Nancy Rue

PUBLISHING
Colorado Springs, Colorado

THE ALLY
Copyright © 1997 by Nancy N. Rue
All rights reserved. International copyright secured.

Library of Congress Cataloging-in-Publication Data
Rue, Nancy N.
  The invasion / Nancy Rue.
    p.   cm.—(Christian heritage series ; 14)
  Summary: Living with his uncle on a South Carolina plantation in 1860, 11-year-old
Austin decides to disobey the law and teach reading to a slave he has befriended, an act
that endangers his friend but prompts his uncle to reconsider the treatment of his slaves.

  ISBN 1-56179-541-0
  [1. Slavery—fiction. 2. Afro-Americans—Fiction. 3. Literacy—Fiction. 4. South
Carolina—Fiction. 5. Christian Life—Fiction.] I. Title. II. Series: Rue, Nancy N.
Christian heritage series; the Charleston years; bk. 14.

PZ7.R88515A1   1997
[Fic]—dc21   97-25411
                                                                          CIP
                                                                           AC

Published by Focus on the Family Publishing,
Colorado Springs, Colorado 80995.

This author is represented by the literary agency of Alive Communications, 1465 Kelly
Johnson Blvd., Suite 320, Colorado Springs, CO 80920.

This is a work of fiction, and any resemblance between the characters in this book and
real persons is coincidental.

Editor: Keith Wall
Cover Design: Bradley Lind
Cover Illustration: Cheri Bladholm

Printed in the United States of America

97 98 99 00/10 9 8 7 6 5 4 3 2 1

*For Wanda Thomas,
my ally.*

Canaan Grove Plantation,
Charleston
1860-1861

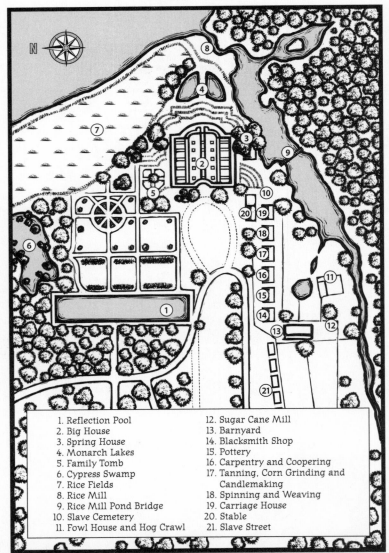

1. Reflection Pool
2. Big House
3. Spring House
4. Monarch Lakes
5. Family Tomb
6. Cypress Swamp
7. Rice Fields
8. Rice Mill
9. Rice Mill Pond Bridge
10. Slave Cemetery
11. Fowl House and Hog Crawl
12. Sugar Cane Mill
13. Barnyard
14. Blacksmith Shop
15. Pottery
16. Carpentry and Coopering
17. Tanning, Corn Grinding and Candlemaking
18. Spinning and Weaving
19. Carriage House
20. Stable
21. Slave Street

"Boy, you don't got to hunker down over the water like the pond gonna get away from you. Set yourself back 'fore you falls in."

Austin Hutchinson grinned at the serious black face of Henry-James. "*That* would be a disaster. Neither one of us can swim!"

Henry-James grunted and settled back against the laurel oak, bobbing his fishing pole in Rice Mill Pond, his legs branching out from his knee-length shirt like two dark logs.

Austin turned to look at his cousin Charlotte Ravenal, who sat on his other side, her blue-plaid day skirt plumped up over her cage crinoline like a mushroom, her cotton stockings crumpled at her side.

"Swimming's about the *only* thing Henry-James can't do," Austin said to her.

Charlotte just nodded as she watched her fishing line between her two pink feet. She didn't talk unless she had something important to say.

1

Not like me, Austin thought. *According to Polly and Aunt Olivia, I hardly ever hush up.* He loosened the foot straps on his trousers and rolled up his tight-fitting pantaloons to his knees. *But there's so* much *to talk about, especially here at Canaan Grove!*

Austin twisted his head, swishing deer-colored hair across his forehead, and took a look at his uncle's South Carolina plantation. Happily, he scanned the blacksmith and carpentry and tanning shops behind them and the Big House and the rice fields beyond.

But he felt himself frowning as his golden-brown eyes took in the slave cemetery and then glanced back toward Slave Street where Henry-James and the other "property" lived.

Austin's Uncle Drayton had 200 slaves he'd purchased or inherited to run his huge rice plantation here on the Ashley River. *Uncle Drayton always called slavery the South's "peculiar institution."*

Austin cringed. He could just hear his hot-tempered abolitionist father roaring, "Call it what it is, Drayton! It's slavery—the cruel and unchristian ownership of other human beings! I don't care how well you treat them, it's still wrong!"

That thought made Austin squirm inside his loose shirt.

How can Uncle Drayton be such a charming man and go to church every Sunday and treat his family like royalty, and still have slaves whose lives he controls—with a whip? Austin had asked himself this question a thousand times since his father had left Austin and his six-year-old brother, Jefferson, and his sickly mother, Sally, here to go on with his anti-slavery work.

"Boy, you better look what you doin' here," Henry-James said.

Austin snapped his attention back to the pond and looked blankly at his friend.

Henry-James was picking lazily at the space between his two front teeth. "You gots that line stuck in them weeds like a fly in molasses."

Austin peered at his fishing line and sighed. It was hopelessly tangled in the tall silky grass that bordered the pond like wild hair.

"If you gonna be catchin' any fish, you got to give attention to what you be doin'," Henry-James said dryly.

He then gave his attention to his own taut line and deftly pulled it out of the water, skimming a wiggling yellow perch across the surface like a beam of sunshine.

"That's your third one today!" Austin said. "I haven't even caught one yet!"

"He deserves it," Charlotte said.

Austin looked back at Henry-James in awe. "That's right! You'll be going out to work in the fields tomorrow." He cocked his head thoughtfully.

"Hold on to your bonnet, Miss Lottie," Henry-James said. "He gonna start askin' questions. Every time he do that with his head, Lord knows we gonna get them questions comin' in like a swarm of bees."

"I just want to know one thing," Austin said.

Henry-James rolled his boot-black eyes at Charlotte, who giggled huskily.

"Does it feel any different being 13?" Austin said. "I'm not even 12 yet, but I want to know, just for future reference."

"Ain't gonna do you no good to be askin' me," Henry-James said in a sour voice. "Your life gonna be all different from mine." He looked away from Austin and set about baiting his hook with a grasshopper.

"We're not so different," Austin insisted. "We're both smart and educated—"

"What you talkin' 'bout?" Henry-James said grimly. "I ain't educated." He tossed his line back out over the water with a jerk.

"I don't mean educated like going-to-school educated," Austin said. "I haven't been to school either. Jefferson and I have always been taught by our mother, since we've been traveling all our lives until we came to Canaan Grove. Even here, Kady is my teacher." He shrugged. "I've heard school is awful and boring anyway. One boy I met in Philadelphia told me his schoolmaster hit his hands with a switch every time he made a mistake on his arithmetic."

"A switch on the hand?" Henry-James said. He made a jeering sound through his lips. "That boy don't know nothin' 'bout whuppin's."

Austin felt his amber eyebrows shoot up. "Do they actually *beat* you when you make a mistake reciting or something?"

Henry-James's dark hands tightened around his fishing pole. "I don't get beat for messin' up my recitin' 'cause there *ain't* no recitin'."

Austin stared. "You mean, you've never had *any* lessons?"

Henry-James shook his closely cropped woolly head.

"Uncle Drayton won't make sure the slave children learn to read and write and cipher?" Austin said indignantly.

"He *can't*," Charlotte said. "It's against the law."

"What law?"

"The Slave Code."

Austin scowled fiercely. "You mean that list of rules that says slaves can't be off the plantation without a pass?"

"That's the one," Charlotte said. She plucked at a long strand of her fawn-colored hair that matched Austin's in hue. "If Daddy breaks that law, he could be put in jail."

"'That which is not just is not law,'" Austin quoted stubbornly. "I learned that from *my* father."

"Well, *your* daddy be livin' in the North where he can say that and don't nobody string him up in a tree for it," Henry-James said.

"But it isn't *fair!*" Austin said. He tossed his pole aside and scrambled up to his knees.

Henry-James shot Charlotte a look. "You got yourself ready for *more* questions, Miss Lottie?"

"I just want to get this straight," Austin said. "You've *never* had any schooling?"

"Nope."

"You can't write your name?"

"I can do that, yessir," Henry-James said, pulling his broad shoulders up stiffly. "Miss Lottie done taught me that— and my alphabet. I knows them letters."

Austin blinked. "That's it? You can't . . . *read?*"

This time Henry-James just shook his head and riveted his eyes on the dimple in the water where his grasshopper floated tauntingly above the fish. Austin felt a poke in his side—from Charlotte.

"Don't," she whispered.

Austin clamped his mouth shut and edged toward the pond bank and began to work at his tangled line.

He couldn't imagine not being able to read! That was the most important thing a person could learn in the Hutchinson household. He and his mother read and talked about books as much as Aunt Olivia and Polly drooled over gowns, gloves, and bonnets—which was enough to create large puddles in the drawing room.

He glowered at the knot of fishing line in his hand.

If I couldn't read and write and think, I'd be practically nothing at all! The thought sent a shiver across his heart.

"I'm telling you, it's a stupid law—a *terrible* law!" he said.

"Well, there ain't nothin' you can do 'bout it, so you might as well quit your fussin'," Henry-James said. "What you gots to do is get your white self back from that water, 'cause I's tellin' *you*, you gonna be in that there pond and ain't nobody gonna be able to save you from drownin'!"

Austin scooted back an inch, but his mind was still spinning.

The black boy was watching him closely. On the other side of him, there was a low, grumbling sound, and a brown head with enough skin for two dogs rose from the grass. Bogie, Henry-James's bloodhoundish mutt, watched Austin intently, too, from the pink-rimmed eyes that winked within the drooping folds of his fur.

"You sees it, too, Bogie," Henry-James said to him.

"Sees what?'" Austin said.

"You sees it, Miss Lottie?"

"I do," Charlotte said. "You know there's going to be trouble when he looks like that."

"Looks like what?" Austin said.

"Like you gots some harebrained idea brewing in that there head of yours."

"Mmmm-hmmm," Charlotte said.

Austin couldn't hold back a grin. It was nice to have other kids know him that well. He'd never had friends like them before, not in his entire life.

That's why this is a wonderful *idea,* he told himself.

We're talking about my friend here!

"Well, come on," Henry-James said. "Let's hear it."

Austin jumped to his feet with his back to the pond. This called for heavy persuasion.

"Be careful now, boy," Henry-James said. "You 'bout to slide right off into that pond yet!"

But Austin ignored him as he chopped at the air for emphasis. "I'm not a Southron," he said, "so I don't have to follow their silly southern laws. *I* think you should learn how to read, and I think *I* should teach you! We could have lessons instead of playing every afternoon. Jefferson has plenty of primers and chapbooks to start with, though I know you're so smart, Henry-James, that you'll be out of those slick as a hog crawl."

Charlotte was already shaking her head until her silky hair swayed, and Henry-James had his lips pulled up to his flat nose.

"Now you jus' hold on, Massa Boston Austin," he said. "First place, I gots to start my workin' as a field hand tomorrow mornin' 'fore the sun come up, and I's workin' till the sun near go down. There ain't gonna be no more playin' for this chil'."

"What about dinnertime?"

"I be carryin' my dinner in a can and leavin' it under a bush in the mornin', and that's where I'll eat come noontime."

"Then we can meet you there and have lessons," Austin said. "And what about at night?"

"When I be workin' in the garden at the cabin?"

"I can sit on the steps and teach while you hoe."

"With my mama right there watchin'?"

Austin paused. "I forgot about Ria. She doesn't like it when we sneak around and break the rules, does she?"

"She don't want no trouble."

"I thought you didn't either, Austin," Charlotte said in her clear voice. "You told me you weren't going to do any more lying and sneaking."

"But this is different!" Austin cried, arms stabbing again.

Austin flailed at the air for the words, his back and legs getting into the action, too. "Uncle Drayton can control what Henry-James does with his body, but he can't control what he does with his mind."

"He *can* and he *do*, every day of my life!" Henry-James said.

Austin leaned back, hand on his forehead in dramatic disbelief. "Is this Henry-James Ravenal talking?"

"Watch it, boy, you gonna—"

"I can't believe it! Henry-James, the boy who talks back to Marse Drayton to defend his grandfather."

"Massa Austin, watch yourself—"

"*Our* Henry-James, who even the old slaves look up to, is going to let a ridiculous law turn his mind into a . . . a *dwarf!*"

Austin gave a loud laugh and threw his head back—just to make it stick in their minds. But with his head went his shoulders, his backbone—and then his legs.

He grabbed at the air—Henry-James lunged forward— and Austin's feet slithered crazily in the mud.

The next thing he knew, his back was hitting the water with a slap, and the sky was disappearing in a watery cloud over his head.

✢ ✦ ✢

Chapter Two

ustin's arms and legs clawed at the pond, his hands reaching up for the surface, his feet groping for the bottom. He couldn't find either one. He opened his mouth to cry out, and it filled with water that surged down his throat and into his chest.

I'm going to drown . . . I'm going to drown . . . I'm going to drown! his mind screamed out to him.

He fought those thoughts with a thrashing of his arms. Somehow that propelled him to the surface, and for a moment his head broke through. The green of the pond grass, the blue of Charlotte's skirt, and the black of Henry-James's face spun together like a sickening kaleidoscope. He gasped and sank back toward the bottom.

Desperately, Austin flapped his arms through the water and kicked his legs. The water fell away again, and once more he broke through the surface and choked to breathe.

"Massa Austin!" he heard a voice cry. "Grab on to—"

But the rest was lost as he plunged once more. Churning

and kicking for all he was worth, Austin got back to the top. He couldn't see anything except the water spraying out in panicked splashing, but he could hear Henry-James's voice.

"The stick, Massa Austin! Grab the stick!"

Austin took another frightening drop. He tried to kick his way up again, but his legs already felt like green beans below him.

I can't drown! Jesus, I can't!

That was right. Pray. He'd learned that.

Lord, please!

He gave his string-bean legs another thrust. This time when the water dropped below his neck, he kept his arms under the water. Heaving for air, he searched the bank, still kicking his legs beneath him. He bobbed up and down, but his head stayed up.

"Grab the stick, Massa Austin!" Henry-James cried.

Austin saw a thick branch stuck out toward him like a rescuing arm. Coughing, he pushed his own arm up and out to it, but several inches of air separated them.

"I'll get closer!" Henry-James called out.

Austin worked his legs like train wheels while Henry-James got on his stomach on the side of the pond.

"Here, Massa Austin!" he cried. "Grab it now!"

He thrust the stick toward Austin, who reached out and felt his hand hit it. His fingers wrapped around it and he clung, his heart hammering the rhythm of relief.

"Don't pull, Massa Austin!" Henry-James shouted. "Just hang—"

But it was too late. Austin felt the branch come free, and he was suddenly clinging to a piece of wood that sank with the weight of his body.

"Lordy!" Henry-James screamed.

It was the first time Austin had ever heard panic in his friend's voice, and it went through him like a candle flame. He flailed his arms instead of his legs, the branch still gripped tightly in his terrified hand and waving uselessly in the air. The water rose to his mouth, his nose, his eyes, and he thrashed wildly.

The water had agitated all the way over his head when Austin suddenly felt a tug at the branch. It jerked and yanked and tugged again. There was something pulling at the branch, hauling him up with it.

Austin's face came through the water, and his chest heaved. Ahead of him, towing him toward the bank with the branch in his mouth and his long ears trailing behind him, was Bogie. Austin hung on to the other end of the stick and floated to shore, half laughing, half crying.

Even as his stomach touched the silty bottom at the pond's edge, Austin felt two sets of hands grabbing his arms and dragging him out of the water. Charlotte and Henry-James beached him on the grass, rolled him over, and stuck their alarmed faces close to his.

"He breathin'?" Henry-James said.

"Yes," Austin said, though he wasn't sure at all. His chest felt as if the entire Ashley River were pressing down on it. He tried to sit up, but another face poked itself against his nose and sniffed.

"Bogie, you're a hero!" Charlotte said.

Bogie responded with a lick that went from Austin's chin to his forehead and back down again. Then he stepped away and shook himself, skin flopping and pond water spewing everywhere. Henry-James scowled ferociously.

"You coulda been drowned, boy!" he said. "When you gonna learn to be more careful with yourself? Next time, I prob'ly won't be here to save you. No sirree, I be out in them fields a-workin', and you be at the bottom of that there pond with them crawdads eatin' on ya."

"Oh, Henry-James!" Charlotte said. She wrinkled up her freckled nose. "That's a horrible thought!"

"It sure 'nuff is." Henry-James pointed a finger at Austin. "Now you watch it, boy."

"You'd better get yourself in and get changed before someone catches you and starts yelling," Charlotte said.

"Will we see you tomorrow?" Austin said as Charlotte peeled his sleeve from his arm and tugged at it. "Shall we meet you for lessons out by the rice field?"

Henry-James studied Austin's face for a moment and then shook his head. "I don't know 'bout that yet, Massa Austin. I just don' know."

It was time for dinner when Austin had finally changed into fresh pantaloons and shirt and talked Polly's slave girl, Tot, into hanging his wet ones by a fire in the kitchen, where Aunt Olivia wouldn't spot them.

When Uncle Drayton finished asking the blessing, Aunt Olivia's large, dark eyes rested grimly on Austin.

"What is that on your hair, Austin Hutchinson?" she said, chin doubling the way it did when she tilted her head to shoot him a miffed look.

"Water," Austin said. Across from him, his 16-year-old cousin Kady was tugging on one of her thick, cocoa-colored curls and watching him with curious amusement in her dark eyes.

"Who instructed you to bathe today?" Aunt Olivia said.

"You have been told that you are only to wash yourself on Saturday. I don't care what you have to do in the North where even the air is filthy—"

"I went for a swim," Austin said.

Aunt Olivia clutched at the cameo at her throat. "Where?"

"In Rice Mill Pond."

Austin felt his face twitching, but he didn't laugh, even when he saw the shimmer in Kady's eyes and the sparkle in Uncle Drayton's. Next to him, 13-year-old Polly screeched, a sound that was automatically echoed by Tot, who was standing behind her.

"The pond!" she cried. "It's completely disgusting in there! The ducks use it as a necessary!"

"Polly, really!" Aunt Olivia put a plump hand over her mouth and turned to Uncle Drayton.

Austin secretly wished Jefferson were here at the table instead of eating up in his mother's bedroom with her. At age six, his favorite subject was "going to the necessary." He could really stir things up with Polly. Last winter, Austin had learned that skinny, brown-toothed Polly had a sharp tongue, but she was harmless. It was actually fun to "squeeze" her until she squeaked.

"I think it's time for a change in topic, don't you?" Uncle Drayton said smoothly. His voice was like honey as usual, although when he was *really* turning on the charm, it was like molasses. Austin felt the mischief drain out of him as he watched his handsome uncle put his fork elegantly into his beef ragout and come up with a cube of meat and a chunk of potato, dripping with sauce.

When I came here, I was so happy I look like him, Austin thought. He poked at a piece of celery in his ragout. *Now I'm not so sure—not after what I heard today.*

"I have some very good news," Uncle Drayton said gaily. "I took our little man out riding today, and I must say he is doing exceptionally well. We'll turn him into a horseman yet."

Uncle Drayton had started calling Jefferson their "little man" since they first arrived.

"Lovely," Aunt Olivia said coldly.

"I'm just sorry he isn't at the table with us so he can bask in the compliments," Uncle Drayton said.

"I'm not!" Polly hitched up her narrow shoulders and tried to toss the curls at the nape of her neck. As usual, they lay there like limp dandelion stems. "I hate it when Jefferson sits at the table with us. There's always silverware on the floor, bits of china under the table—"

"What are you complaining about?" Kady said dryly. "It seems to me you're the one who was assigned to look after him, and lately Daddy has been doing all your work for you."

"It's high time *someone* relieved me of some of my drudgery."

"I just received a letter from Jefferson Davis today," Uncle Drayton cut in quickly.

"Jefferson Davis, the congressman from Mississippi?" Austin said.

"You *would* know that, Boston Austin," Polly murmured under her breath. "You know everything else."

"He and I fought together in Mexico some years ago," Uncle Drayton said. "A finer man I have never met."

"He's one of the few men you'd ever take advice from," Aunt Olivia said proudly. "You're such a strong individual, Drayton—never swayed by other men's opinions."

"Really?" The edge in Kady's voice brought all heads up.

She was glaring coldly down the table at her father.

"I believe that is so, yes," said Uncle Drayton.

"I've always thought you went along with whatever the rest of the planters decided," Kady said.

"Kady!" Aunt Olivia said, her eyes showing her shock. "I have told you time and again never to argue with a man about political matters. It's so unbecoming to a lady."

"Let her speak, Olivia," Uncle Drayton said. He stroked the neat fringe of whiskers along his chin.

Good, Austin thought, pretending to chase a piece of carrot across his plate with his fork. *I've been trying to figure Kady out ever since I came here. Does she support her father—or is she an abolitionist, like us?*

"It just seems to me," Kady said gravely, "that you always go along with popular opinion."

Aunt Olivia gasped, but Uncle Drayton held up his hand to silence her. "Go on," he said. The gleam was gone from his eyes.

"Take the Slave Code, for instance," Kady said. "If it had been left up to you alone, would you have decided to install the Patty Roller system or refuse the slaves an education?"

"You know what the reasons are," Uncle Drayton said.

"I don't," said Austin.

"Nor do you need to," Aunt Olivia snapped.

"I'm sure you've read about the slave rebellions and uprisings," Uncle Drayton said. "Those escapes happen only when slaves read some of the anti-slavery literature put out by—" he stopped, and then said "—people like your father."

Austin's neck stiffened, and he looked Uncle Drayton in the eye. "Could Seton read?" he said.

Drayton's eyebrows went up. "Seton!"

"He escaped a few months ago. Was it because he could read?"

"No!" Uncle Drayton said, voice blaring like a silver trumpet. And then he closed his eyes for an instant and forced his voice to be smooth and deep again. "Like most of his black brothers, Seton was actually quite stupid. He allowed himself to be caught."

"He was caught, Drayton?" Aunt Olivia cried. "When? You didn't tell me!"

"I just learned of it this morning."

"Is he to be returned to us, then?"

"I wouldn't have him on my land again if he were the last slave in the South," Uncle Drayton said tightly. "I made an arrangement with . . ."

But Austin didn't hear the rest. A deep shiver had torn through his heart.

Seton, caught? What did that mean? That he was being held captive in some prison? Being beaten? Picking cotton on some broiling Georgia cotton plantation when he was used to tending to Uncle Drayton here in this elegant house?

Austin felt himself sag. He hadn't known his uncle's body slave very long, but he'd liked him as much as he did Henry-James and Charlotte. Seton had been kind to him when no one else seemed to understand him. The news made him put down his fork and push away the dish of Brown Betty, his favorite dessert.

"Seton left because he was miserable," Kady was saying.

"Indeed!" Aunt Olivia said indignantly. "After all your father did for him!"

"Such as?"

Aunt Olivia didn't answer her. She just turned with fury

on her face to her husband. "I know where this comes from, Drayton," she said. "I warned you about her spending so much time upstairs with Sally Hutchinson, reading those books and talking nonsense."

"Aunt Sally and I talk about nothing so nonsensical as you and Polly do," Kady said calmly. "With all your intellectual discussions about hoop skirts and face paint."

Polly sat up straight as a clothespin. "Face paint? What would I know about face paint?"

"You're wearing it now, aren't you?" Kady said. "I've never known your cheeks to have quite such a rosy glow."

Austin peered closely at Polly. On careful inspection, her skin did appear to be stained with something. He sniffed.

"That's beet juice, isn't it?" he said. "That's awfully clever, Polly—"

"No, it is not!"

"Drayton, I implore you to forbid Kady to spend any more time with your sister. She is twisting the girl's mind!"

"You haven't answered my question, Daddy. Would you have formed that Slave Code on your own—without your cronies?"

"I follow the lead of only one man besides myself—and that is Jefferson Davis! As long as he continues to own slaves and fights for the right to do so, so shall I!"

The madness clamored back and forth across the table. For once, Austin didn't say a word. He only looked across at Charlotte, who was looking back at him. He saw her nod ever so slightly, and he knew she was thinking just what he was.

✝ ✝ ✝

Chapter Three

There was still the matter of the promise Austin had made to himself last winter. That was what nagged at the back of his mind like a pesky little brother as he climbed the front staircase after dinner.

What about no more lying to Uncle Drayton? his thoughts pestered him. *And no more sneaking around because we're disobeying his orders?*

But what about how unfair this all is? said some even louder thoughts. *What about Henry-James not knowing how to read? What about him ending up like Seton?*

There was only one place to take questions like that.

Sally Hutchinson was propped up, book in hand, on one of the wing-backed chairs situated in front of her fireplace. Like Austin, Charlotte, and Uncle Drayton, she looked like a Ravenal with her hair the color of a deer and her eyes amber-brown. Jefferson, who looked more like a Hutchinson, was on the floor at her feet, engrossed in a toy. His dark, tousled head was bent toward the thing, and over his sizzling blue

18

eyes, his rosy forehead was furrowed like the rows in Henry-James's garden. He didn't look up when Austin came in, which was fine with Austin. The only person who could talk more than Austin was his brother.

"How was dinner?" Mother said.

"Like usual," Austin said.

"Ah, plenty of silly fussing and fighting, I take it."

Austin slumped into the other chair and swung his feet back and forth over the oriental rug. If Aunt Olivia were here, she'd be turning 10 shades of scarlet—which at the moment was precisely why he was doing it.

"It wasn't just *silly* fussing," Austin said. "It was . . . hateful."

Mother set her book down and looked closely at Austin. "Talk," she said.

"Did you know that it's against the Slave Code for the slaves to learn to read and write?"

She nodded solemnly. "That's one of the things your father and I hate the most about slavery."

"I should have listened more closely to Father's lectures," Austin said.

"Oh, you were much too young. And besides, you were always kept too busy watching—" She pointed silently to Jefferson, who was scowling intently at his toy.

"It isn't right," Austin said.

"It's abominable."

Austin squirmed impatiently in the chair.

His mother watched him. "There's something brewing in that wonderful head of yours," she said as she set the glass down on the polished cherry table.

"I want to teach Henry-James to read, but it's against the rules—*their* rules."

"Rules *we* don't believe in."

Austin looked at her quickly. "So it's all right for us to break them?"

"I see your problem," Mother said thoughtfully. "If you're going to do this, you'll have to lie to Uncle Drayton and go behind his back, which you decided you weren't going to do anymore."

"Then you think I shouldn't do it."

"I didn't say that. But if it's discovered that one of Uncle Drayton's slaves has been educated—*with* his knowledge—he could get into a great deal of trouble."

"Charlotte said he'd go to jail."

"I'm afraid so. And there's someone else you have to protect, too."

"Who?" Austin said.

"Charlotte." Mother cocked her head sadly. "She can't be part of this."

Austin felt his chest tighten. "Why not?"

"Because Uncle Drayton is her father. It would be wrong for you to ask her to disobey her father."

To Austin's surprise, his mother's eyes grew moist. "But you may be Henry-James's only chance." She laced and unlaced her fingers in her lap. "When Ria and I were little girls, I taught her everything I was learning from our governess. She learned so fast—I always knew she was much smarter than I was." She looked mistily into the fireplace. "The only time my father ever whipped me was when he found out. That was the end of the lessons. Ria never got another chance."

"You could teach her now. She's your nurse."

Sally shook her head. "Ria is too afraid."

"Of what?"

"Of doing something to make Drayton so angry that he would sell her away from her father and Henry-James."

"He would never do that!" Austin cried. "I can't believe he'd be that cruel—"

"This is a stupid toy!" a high-pitched voice broke in. "I hate it!"

Austin felt something hard hit him on the shoulder.

"Ow!"

"It's hateful!"

"You didn't have to throw it at me!"

Austin leaned over and picked up a wooden box with a handle on top, and Mother turned an astonished face on Jefferson.

"Why did you do that?" she said.

"Because I've been playing with it all this long time, and it doesn't do anything!"

Austin plunked the box on the table. "Of course it doesn't do anything, shrimp. It's called a Do-Nothing Box. The whole idea is to think up something to do with it—besides hurl it at me." Austin rolled his eyes. "You have no imagination."

"I do so!" Jefferson protested. "I imagine Maximillian all the time."

Austin and his mother looked at each other blankly.

"What's a Maximillian?" Austin asked.

"It's not a *what*—it's a *who*," Jefferson said.

"Then *who* is he, dear?" Mother said patiently. Austin could never understand how she could be that calm when the boy was so infuriating. "Do I know him?"

"Of *course* you don't know him," Jefferson said in

disgust. "He's in *my* imagination."

"Oh, an imaginary friend," Sally said. "I see."

"I don't," Austin said. "What good is a friend who isn't real?"

"He's real!"

Mother sent Austin a warning look, but Austin knew he could get away with one more question.

"How can he be real if you can't see or hear him—or touch him?" he said.

"Because," Jefferson said, setting his very-red lips, "I *believe* he's real."

"That's good enough for me," his mother said, looking firmly at Austin. "Why don't you and Maximillian run into the nursery and get those alphabet blocks you found? We'll teach little Max some new words."

"All right," Jefferson said, blue eyes round and serious, "but he doesn't like to be called Max, and he isn't little." He looked at Austin and haughtily tilted his chin. "He's *much* bigger than Austin."

He marched from the room, nearly plowing down a tall black woman in the doorway. Ria, Henry-James's mother, watched him with a suggestion of amusement in her eyes. She didn't smile, of course. Like her son, she seldom did.

Austin sighed. He knew it wouldn't be a good idea to talk about Henry-James's reading lessons in front of Ria. No, the next thing to do was to find Charlotte, and he wasn't looking forward to it. She wasn't going to like what he had to tell her.

She was waiting for him on one of the two grand staircases that curved away from each other like wings in the back hall of the Big House.

"Where can we go to talk?" Austin whispered to her.

Her brown eyes gleamed, and she nodded her silky head toward the door. "Follow me," she said.

She led him merrily outside, the day alive with new fruit blossoms, recently hatched buckeye butterflies, and Carolina wrens and mockingbirds and chickadees celebrating spring with a chorus of warbles and chirps. The two children splashed through several luscious puddles and darted down a dozen sand-covered paths bordered with azaleas before Charlotte settled on a poplar in the formal gardens.

She scampered up it like a squirrel. It took Austin longer, but he managed to lumber his way up and settle beside her on a thick branch without ripping either his trousers or his skin. That was progress.

"Well?" she said. She was never one to waste words.

"I'm going to teach Henry-James to read."

Her face broke into a smile that crinkled her nose. "When do we start?"

Austin fixed his eyes uneasily on an empty squirrel's nest. "Well, I wanted to talk to you about that," he said.

"So talk. Nothing's ever been able to stop you before."

But knowing how mad you'll be when I tell you that you can't help me might keep me quiet, Austin thought, stomach churning.

"Uh-oh," she said suddenly. She was pointing across the garden.

Austin followed her finger with his eyes. "Is that Kady?"

"Yes."

"Why is she all dressed up? Who is that with her?"

Charlotte put her finger to her lips and leaned in to whisper. "A beau Mama arranged."

"Does Kady like him?"

"No! She says he's just looking for a rich wife."

"A wife!" Austin cried, just before plastering his hand over his mouth.

Charlotte nodded. "Kady was so mad she threw her hairbrush across the room."

Austin watched the couple come down the path between two rows of crepe myrtles. The trees were a blaze of pink, but Kady's face was a portrait in gray. Her hand hung limply on the arm of a thin man with buckteeth, wearing a brown frock coat.

"His teeth are awfully big," Austin whispered to Charlotte.

She covered her mouth, but her eyes sparkled. Kady and Big-Teeth settled on a bench by the pool, and Austin could almost hear *her* molars grinding. Big-Teeth couldn't have heard it. He was filling the air with the sound of his own voice.

But both Charlotte and Austin heard another sound, footsteps, coming from the direction of the formal gardens. Austin gasped when he saw who it was.

Polly, gowned in blue-green silk taffeta with huge puffed sleeves and even more monstrous bows across the bottom, was picking her way along the path with Tot stumbling behind her and holding up the cumbersome skirt—so high that Polly's embroidered cotton drawers were on display for all to see.

Polly had no idea. She was busy waving a Chantilly lace fan in front of her face and trying to bounce her limp curls. She was headed straight for Kady and her caller.

"She's going to show off for Kady's beau," Charlotte whispered. "Look, she's powdered her face this time."

"With what?"

Charlotte stifled a giggle. "Crushed egg shells. She had Tot spend all morning making it."

Austin wrinkled his nose. "That's disgusting!"

Below them, Polly came within several yards of the couple and stopped, fan to her chest, and gasped.

"Oh, my!" she cried. "I'm so sorry. I had no idea you two were out here." She fanned herself coquettishly, eyes batting in time.

"Uh-*huh*," Kady said dryly. She glared at Polly, but even as she did, a gleam came into her eyes that Austin could see from his perch in the tree. "I'm so glad you came by, Polly!" she burst out suddenly in a too-cheerful voice. "I'd like for you to meet Yates Lawrence. Mr. Lawrence, my sister Polly! Perhaps she could join us!"

Yates looked less than overjoyed to see Polly, but once she recovered from the shock of Kady's welcome, Polly rose to the occasion. She fanned and batted and curtsied and even reached into the bodice of her gown and pulled out a handkerchief, which she immediately dropped on the ground.

"Oh, my. How clumsy of me!" she said.

Yates dutifully got up to fetch it for her. Austin choked.

"Why, thank you, kind sir," Polly said, still aquiver. "You're a gentleman, is what."

Yates nodded absently and looked quickly down at Kady. "Miss Kady, I would much rather be alone. If you'll excuse us, Miss Molly."

Kady rose as if she were headed for the hangman's noose, and Polly stood still as a post.

"Of course," Polly said stiffly. "You all just go on ahead

now and enjoy this beautiful day."

Which Yates proceeded to do, leading Kady around a hedge and off into the formal gardens. As soon as they were out of sight, Polly hissed after them, "And it's *Polly!* Pollyanna Olivia Ravenal!" She hurled her fan to the ground and stomped her foot, bringing it down squarely on Tot's toe. The slave girl squealed and Polly turned to her, face redder than after her application of beet juice.

"What are *you* yelling about?" she shouted at Tot. *"I'm* the one who was just treated like the dirt on the bottom of someone's shoe! My own sister!"

Austin couldn't take any more. His laughter squirted through the fingers clamped over his mouth, filling the gardens with an echoing guffaw. Charlotte's giggles rose above his own.

Polly's neck jerked back, and she glared up at the tree. "You!" she shrieked.

"Let's go!" Charlotte hissed to Austin.

She swung down to the next branch and dropped lightly to the ground. She was already disappearing into a grove of cherry trees by the time Austin managed to crawl out of the poplar and fall to the sand. All the while, Polly was screeching, with Tot parroting every sound.

"You were spying on me! I'll get you! I'll get you both!"

Austin started to pull himself up, but a claw snatched at the back of his shirt.

"If you think I'm not going to tell my mother about this, you've got another thing coming, Mr. Boston Austin!"

Austin couldn't answer her for laughing. He tugged gleefully at his shirt, but she hung on like a vice.

"Oh, no," she said, "you're not going anywhere except

straight to the house, where I will tell—"

"That you caught us while you were parading around out here for Kady's beau?" said a voice from the edge of the trees.

Charlotte stood there, out of breath but grinning. Austin grinned, too.

"That's right," he said, "and in egg shell powder, no less. We can tell her we were barely able to save you from being attacked by hungry pigs."

Austin felt the claws unfold from his blouse and heard the silk taffeta rustle furiously.

"Don't you worry—either of you!" Polly spat through her teeth. "I'll get you somehow!"

She swished off in a huff with poor Tot jogging to keep up with her. Charlotte chuckled from deep in her throat.

"We really are a great team, you and I, Boston," she said as she watched them go. "There isn't anything we can't do together."

⚜ ⚜ ⚜

Chapter Four

Charlotte was so delighted for the rest of the afternoon at having yet another thing to hang over Polly's head that she seemed to forget about Henry-James's reading lessons.

I'm sure not going to remind her! Austin thought that night as he lay in bed beside the sleeping Jefferson. His thoughts were too busy to let him drift off.

Had his mother's father actually whipped her for teaching Ria to read? Would Uncle Drayton do that to Charlotte?

Austin shuddered. There was only one thing to do—and that was to give Henry-James his lessons without telling Charlotte. He'd just have to come up with a plan to make it work.

Which was easier to say than to do. He and Charlotte had lessons together with Kady every morning, and they always went from there to dinner with their heads bent close in chatter. If he suddenly disappeared, Charlotte would want to know why.

Then a miracle happened, and strangely enough it was announced by Polly. At eleven o'clock the next morning, she pushed open the music room door during lessons and thrust her brassy head in.

"Good morning!" Kady said. "I'm glad you came in. I wanted to talk to you about what happened yesterday—"

"Well, *I* don't want to talk to *you*—ever again," Polly said coldly. "I only came to tell you that you and Charlotte are to go upstairs and dress. Father has a photographer coming to take a family portrait, and it has to be done at high noon when the light is good or some such. Dinner will be later."

"What about me?" Austin said—casually.

Polly lifted her upper lip. "I said it was a *family* portrait."

Any other time, that would have stabbed Austin to the heart, but this time, he had a hard time keeping a smile from taking over his face.

"That was mean of her," Charlotte said to him when Polly was gone.

"I'll get over it," Austin said. He tried not to sound too cheerful. "I hate to get dressed up anyway. Just meet me at the pond when you're finished."

He waited until she'd disappeared upstairs before he tore out the back door and flew toward the rice fields.

Uncle Drayton had a thousand acres of rice fields, and they had all been plowed in March in preparation for the seed that would produce a million pounds of rice this year. Austin had spent hours watching the oxen pull the plows, fitted with their special boots for the soft, boggy earth. Then he'd witnessed the slave men and women breaking up dirt clods and leveling the surface and digging foot-deep trenches, all with their eight-inch hoes, singing their glorious work songs.

Austin had read all about rice cultivation, and he knew that now that it was April, the slaves would be working from the time Daddy Elias blew his horn at sunrise until the sun went down in the evening to get the fields all planted before the first of May.

He reached the top of a knoll and looked down over the sea of muddy trenches, dotted with black heads and seed baskets. The slaves moved gracefully across to the rhythm of their song:

I want to be an angel, and with an angel stand,
A crown upon my forehead, a harp within my hand.
Right there before my Savior, so glorious and so bright,
I'll hear the sweetest music, and praise Him day and night.

There were plenty of shouts of "Hallelujah, brother!" and "Praise the Lord," and Austin closed his eyes and rocked with the people. *They always make Jesus seem so real,* he thought.

And then he shook himself and looked for Henry-James. It wasn't hard to find his sturdy figure. He was close by, behind some of the more experienced slaves, with his snowy-haired grandfather Daddy Elias walking beside him.

"I'm so proud of you," Austin had told Henry-James when he had announced he was now 13 and would start working the fields.

"I ain't nothin' special," Henry-James had grumbled. "I's just a half-hand at first. I only gots to sow a quarter acre in a day. And Daddy 'Lias, he'll be watchin' me for to make sure I's doin' it good enough."

"You do everything good enough!" Austin had protested.

But Henry-James had gone on to explain that there was a special way to plant seed rice—the way their ancestors had done it in Africa.

Austin felt his chest swell now as he watched Henry-James press a hole in the trench with his heel, drop in some seed, and cover it with his foot. *He makes it look just like a dance,* Austin thought proudly. *Look there—Daddy Elias hardly has to tell him anything.*

Uncle Drayton didn't hire white overseers the way some of the planters did. He gave his oldest, most trusted slaves that work, and Daddy Elias was one of those.

And someday Henry-James will be, too, Austin thought happily.

And then he tripped over his own thoughts.

I don't want Henry-James to be an overseer when he's an old man! I don't want him to be a slave at all!

Which was exactly why he was here. The minute Daddy Elias blew his horn for dinnertime, Austin charged down the hill and grabbed Henry-James by the arm as soon as he stepped off the field and put his basket down.

It was only then that Austin noticed his head was glistening with sweat and his face sagged like Bogie's always did.

"Are you sick?" Austin said.

"No, boy," Henry-James said. "I's tired."

Austin followed him toward a tangle of brush at the edge of the field.

"It's hard work, isn't it?" Austin said sympathetically.

"It ain't like what I's used to, that's for sure 'nuff," Henry-James said. "'T'ain't like sweepin' yards and carryin' water and milkin' cows."

Austin leaned close to him as they walked. "You won't have to do it forever," he whispered. "That's why I'm going to teach you to read."

Henry-James turned to answer him, but just ahead, from within the scrub brush, they heard a low growling sound.

"That's Bogie!" Austin said.

"It is. He in there doin' his job like I tol' him."

"What job?" Austin said.

Henry-James pushed back the underbrush. There sat Bogie with a can between his front paws.

"What's in that?" Austin said.

"My dinner," Henry-James said. "And Bogie, he guardin' it so won't nobody get it 'fore I gets here."

Austin reached down to scratch behind one of the floppy ears, and Bogie looked at him suspiciously.

"It's jus' Massa Austin," Henry-James said. "He ain't gonna take none of it."

Still, Bogie placed himself between the two boys when they sat on the ground and kept a wary eye on Austin.

Henry-James pulled a piece of cornbread out of the can, dipped it into what Austin recognized as Ria's rice-boiled-with-salt-pork, and took a bite. He did that several times before he said a word.

He eats that like he's starving to death! Austin thought.

"So what's this 'bout you teachin' me to read?" Henry-James said finally.

Austin filled him in excitedly. He grinned when he was finished. "We can start right now—today," he said.

But Henry-James shook his head.

"Why not?" Austin said.

"Because I don't want no trouble for Miss Lottie."

"Miss Lott—Charlotte doesn't need to know about it," Austin said.

Henry-James grunted and shoveled in another bite of dripping cornbread. "And how you think you gonna keep this from her?"

Austin frowned. "I haven't figured that out yet, but I will—"

"And what you gonna do if she find out—and she come to you with them eyes all swimmin' in tears and her heart all broke to pieces 'cause you done left her out?"

Austin stiffened so he wouldn't shiver. "That isn't going to happen," he said. "By the time she ever finds out, you'll be reading like Frederick Douglass, and she'll be too proud of you to be mad."

"Who Frederick Douglass?" Henry-James said, scowling. Bogie sniffed doubtfully at Austin.

"He was a slave up in Maryland. His mistress taught him to read and write and then he escaped on a ship to Massachusetts. He had his own anti-slavery newspaper and everything." Austin felt his brain twinkle with an idea, and he lowered his voice importantly. "He's the champion of your people, my father says. You could be just like him—even better—and then wouldn't Charlotte be proud?"

Austin watched him closely. Just as he'd hoped, the black boy's eyes lit up like gas lamps. Slowly, he began to nod.

"All right, Massa Austin," he said. "You find you a way to give me lessons without Miss Lottie findin' out, and I'll learn to read circles 'round you."

Austin let out a whoop that brought Bogie to his feet, howling.

"You even got Bogie singin'!" Henry-James said. And then he gave one of his rare smiles.

When the horn blew for Henry-James to return to work, Austin promised to meet him as soon as the moon came up and he was out planting snap beans in their garden.

"How soon you think I can read the Bible to Daddy 'Lias?" Henry-James said as Austin walked him back to the rice field.

Austin thought a minute as he watched the slaves pick up their baskets and head back down the trenches. "By the time the rice is all planted," he said.

Henry-James nodded, and his step was light as he returned to his trench with his basket on his shoulder.

The photo-taking session lasted longer than anyone suspected, what with a small explosion beneath the photographer's black cloth and his singed hair to be tended to and all. By the time a breathless Charlotte met Austin at the pond, she was so full of stories about the sap of grape vines Polly had rubbed around her eyes—supposedly to make them sparkle for the picture—she didn't mention a word about the reading lessons.

This is all going to work out somehow, Austin thought. And after supper and his reading session with his mother and the wrestling match he had to go through to get Jefferson into bed and sleeping, he headed hopefully down the dirt road for Slave Street.

The fires flickering through the glassless windows of the rows of two-room cabins looked as cheerful as Austin felt as he opened the gate to Henry-James's cabin and joined him in the vegetable garden. It was a soft night, and Daddy Elias had pulled a bench out onto the porch and was contentedly watching Henry-James drop seeds into the ground. The boy's shoulders looked heavy with the endless day of working, but when he looked up and saw Austin, they straightened up.

"What I got to learn first, Massa Austin?" he said.

Austin glanced quickly at Daddy Elias. The old man was his best friend on the plantation—next to Henry-James and Charlotte, of course. He hadn't thought about what his reaction would be to the reading lessons.

"It's all right," Henry-James said. "I done tol' him."

"You go on and teach that boy," Daddy Elias said, smiling his spoon-shaped smile at Austin. "Then when I gets old, he can read me the Bible till I goes to the Lord."

"All right," said Austin happily. He reached under his blouse and pulled out a stack of large cards. "This is how we taught Jefferson to read. I'll hold up a card and while you look at it, I'll tell you what it says. We'll do that over and over until you can read them every time you see them."

Henry-James set his mouth in concentration, and Austin held up the first card.

"I don't see no words," he said. "All's I see is a picture."

"The picture is to help you remember—the word is on the other side," Austin said. "What's it a picture of?"

Henry-James peered at it through the darkness. "That there is some kinda strange lookin' boat, Massa Austin."

"No," Austin said. He tried to sound patient like his mother. "It's an ark."

"Let me see that!" Daddy Elias exclaimed. "I always wondered what Marse Noah's boat look like."

Austin handed him the card, which he studied carefully while Austin held up the next one. Once again, Henry-James frowned.

"I ain't never seed nothin' like that there," he said.

"It's a top," Austin said. "Haven't you ever played with one?"

Henry-James shook his head. "Ain't never had no toys, Massa Austin. But let me see that word."

Austin turned the card over, and Henry-James looked at it for so long that Austin thought he might burn a hole in it with his eyes. His mouth formed the word *Top*, popping the P like corn in a fire.

"All right. I got that one," he said suddenly. "Give me the next one."

Austin held one up, and Henry-James gave a happy snort. "Hey, Bogie!" he said. "That there is a picture of you!"

"It's *Dog*," Austin said.

"That don't look like Bogie to me," said a voice from the gate.

Austin watched as Ria approached them, her stern eyes aimed at Henry-James. He shrugged and took a new interest in the seeds in his hand. Austin took that opportunity to slip the cards back under his blouse.

"Did Justine have that baby already?" Daddy Elias said.

Tall, slender Ria gave Henry-James another long look before she turned to Daddy Elias and joined him on the bench.

"She had her a sweet baby girl," Ria said. She wearily pushed back a clump of her wiry hair. "Another piece of property for Marse Drayton."

"Look like bringin' her into the world done wore you out," Daddy Elias said.

Ria didn't answer, and her gaze drifted back to her son. His eyes were directed toward the ground.

"*You* don't seem too wore out for somebody been workin' all day," she said. "You got enough left for to be lookin' at pictures."

"I thought it might help him pass the time while he's planting," Austin said.

"Mmmm-hmmm," she said. Her tone was flat as a plank.

It made Austin clear his throat. "I'd best be getting back," he said. He hoped he didn't sound as nervous as he suddenly felt.

We're going to have to be really careful around her, Austin thought as he made his way across the lawn toward the Big House. *If she tells Henry-James he can't have reading lessons, we'll have to stop. He can't disobey his mother.*

He was deep in a pile of ideas about how to get around Ria as he headed toward the back porch. Before he took his first step up, both feet flew out from under him, and he tumbled backward onto the grass with something wiry—and angry—wrapped around his legs.

"You were down at Henry-James's cabin, weren't you?" Charlotte hissed to him in the dark. She rolled him over and wrestled him to his back, and he was too stunned to even squirm. She planted her hands on his shoulders and looked fiercely into his face.

"You were teaching him to read!" she said. "I know you were doing it—without me!"

✝ ⚜ ✝

Chapter Five

"Let me up and I'll explain!" Austin said.

She leaned on his shoulders until Austin wheezed.

"You were teaching him to read already, weren't you? Tell me the truth!"

"I was—only, Charlotte, let me tell you why!"

But Charlotte gave his shoulders a smack with the heels of both hands and scrambled up. She turned to march up the steps, and Austin snatched at the bottom of her skirt. Several leaves floated to the ground.

"Were you in a tree?" Austin said. "You were spying on me!"

"You were sneaking!"

"I was not! I was only trying to protect you from getting in trouble!"

"She's already *in* trouble, far as I can see."

They both whirled to see Polly and Tot approaching them from the direction of the kitchen building, recently rebuilt

38

after last winter's fire. In spite of the warmth of the April evening, Polly was wearing a long cape with a hood falling down over her forehead.

"Why am I in trouble?" Charlotte said.

"Because you're wandering around out here at night, without permission, I'm sure."

"So are you," Charlotte said.

Polly sniffed from somewhere inside the hood. "Mama said I could go down to the kitchen with Tot."

"Surely you weren't cooking in there?" Austin said.

"If you must know," Polly said in an icy voice, "I've decided that if I'm to begin taking beaus soon, I ought to learn more about how a plantation mistress runs her household."

"In case Yates Lawrence rushes to propose," Austin said, keeping his face straight.

Charlotte giggled.

"What is so funny about that?" Polly said, turning on her like an angry goose. "You saw for yourself how he fetched my handkerchief for me."

"I did see that, didn't you, Charlotte?" Austin said.

"I did," said Charlotte. "Was that before or after he called you by the wrong name?"

"I liked you better when you were a stupid little mouse!" Polly cried. She glared at Austin. "Before *he* came!"

"Better a mouse than a brown-toothed *rat* like you!" Charlotte said.

Polly screamed and lunged at her sister, grabbing Charlotte's nose with her fingers and pulling it like a piece of taffy. Charlotte gave a nasal cry.

Austin grabbed for Polly and caught a handful of cloth.

He gave it a yank, and her hood came off. With another scream, more hideous than the first, she let go of Charlotte and pawed her hands around to flip it back on again.

But she didn't get it in place before Austin saw her hair. Charlotte saw it, too, and she let out a delighted shriek.

"Boston!" she cried. "Did you see that?"

"Good heavenly days, Miss Polly!" Austin shouted gleefully. "Did you know your hair has turned *green?*"

"It is *not* green!"

Tot looked at her dully and nodded her head.

"Of course it is!" said Charlotte. "Even Tot says so."

Polly screamed yet again, this time at poor Tot, who alternated between nodding and shaking her head with a most bewildered look in her black eyes.

"That's what you were doing in the kitchen!" Austin said. "You were trying to dye your hair!"

"Was she really?" Charlotte said.

"I've read about it," said Austin. "You steep black tea for a day, and it darkens your hair."

Polly stopped screaming and stared at him. *"Black* tea?" She whirled on Tot. "Was it *black* tea you used?" she said, her voice winding up.

"Black," Tot said. But she was shaking her head.

Austin's own head was shaking—with laughter. "She used green tea, sure as we're standing here, Polly," he said. "That's the kind Aunt Olivia had for breakfast this morning. I know because I took some up to my mother."

"You are a senseless, stupid piece of *stone!*" Polly shrieked at her beloved Tot. She hurled herself at the poor black girl with her fingernails bared like a cat's claws. Charlotte caught Polly around the waist from behind.

"If you'll stop screaming for a minute, I'll tell you what to do!" Austin shouted in her face. "Just mix an egg in water and scrub it into your hair and rinse it off. All that green will be gone—"

Polly snatched herself away from Charlotte and with a final, blood-freezing scream, marched up the steps and into the house with Tot limping along behind.

"—in a day or two," Austin finished when she was gone.

Then he doubled over at the waist. Through his own guffaws, he could hear Charlotte giggling up and down the scale.

She grabbed Austin's hand and dragged him up the steps and into the house. They smothered their giggles until they got to the second floor and stumbled, hysterical, into Austin's room.

"We got her!" Austin whispered.

"I told you before, Austin, we're a good team. It's going to take both of us to teach Henry-James to read and keep my daddy from finding out."

Austin felt his laughter slip sadly away. "You can't disobey him, Charlotte. You'll get into so much trouble, and I would never forgive myself."

"Not if he doesn't find out."

"No."

"You can't do it by yourself," she said stubbornly. "I don't care how smart you are—you need me to help. And I *have* to. Henry-James is . . . well, he's almost like my brother."

There was no talking her out of it, Austin could see that. But the thought of Uncle Drayton pulling out a whip and—

Jefferson suddenly churned on the bed. "Stupid toy," he murmured in his sleep. He started to sit up, and Austin went for him. His foot came down on something hard and sharp.

"Ow!" he yelped.

Charlotte hopped toward the bed and put her arms around Jefferson. He fell sleepily back to the pillow. Austin leaned over and picked up a block. A big red J with the word "joy" printed under it seemed to stare back at him.

He thought for a moment, then looked at Charlotte with wide eyes.

"Charlotte," he whispered. "I think I might have an idea. Let's go talk to Kady."

They put their plan into effect the next morning. While Charlotte and Austin packed a bundle filled with word cards and alphabet blocks, Kady did some legwork of her own. She entered the music room at eleven o'clock with her eyes shining and her thick, brunette curls bouncing merrily at the base of her neck.

"Lessons out in the garden every day as long as the weather holds," she said triumphantly, "and a picnic basket ready with your dinner every morning. You'll have one today—well, in just a few minutes."

"How did you do that?" Austin said.

She shrugged. "I had to promise Mama I would see another one of her 'prospects' this week."

"Another beau?" Charlotte said. "Oh, Kady, no! You hate that!"

"I'll bear it somehow," she said. "It's for a good cause. I wish I could help you with the teaching, but I'll have to come back here for dinner. It would be much too suspicious, my being there with you children."

"You're helping a lot already," Austin said. "What about Polly?"

Kady's mouth twitched. "She was in the nursery with Jefferson, wearing the most interesting scarf arrangement on her head. Anyway, she was overjoyed to let me take Jefferson off her hands at dinnertime every day. I told her you two would bring him to me, and after this she should bring him to the big oak near the rice field." She shook her head. "Poor Polly. As if the beet juice odor weren't bad enough, this morning she smelled for all the world like raw eggs. What that girl won't do to try to be beautiful."

There was no time to savor that delight with so much work to be done. The minute the bell rang for dinner, Austin and Charlotte raced to the kitchen building for their first picnic basket, stuffed their bundle of teaching tools into it, grabbed Jefferson from the nursery, and were off for the rice fields, skirts, shirts, and feet flying.

"Why are we having a picnic?" Jefferson asked as he hammered his little legs into the ground to keep up.

"We're going to teach you some more reading out here, shrimp," Austin said.

"I know enough reading."

"Henry-James will be there."

"I guess I could learn some more."

"That's what I thought," Austin said. He grinned over his head at Charlotte. The thought of being with Henry-James or Daddy Elias was enough to get Jefferson to do just about anything.

Henry-James was waiting eagerly at the edge of the rice field, but his face sagged when he saw Charlotte.

"I done tol' you, Massa Austin—" he started to say.

But Austin cheerfully hoisted Jefferson up onto his shoulders and said, "We're going to be teaching *Jefferson* more about reading every day at dinnertime," he said cheerfully. "We thought you might like to watch."

"That isn't against the law," Charlotte said. She tossed her silky head. "We even have Mama's permission."

Henry-James looked at each of them in turn, and his eyes took on a knowing glow. "I reckon I better set by and watch, then," he said. "Jus' to be sure none of you all gets bit by no snakes or bugs."

"Absolutely," Austin said.

And so it was—every day that glorious April of 1860.

Kady, Charlotte, and Austin had their lessons under a big oak near the river in the mornings whenever it didn't rain. They read *Idylls of the King* and figured long division—and planned the day's lesson for "Jefferson." Kady sat next to the stuffed picnic basket and helped with a few tricks she'd learned while teaching Charlotte to read.

With the dinner bell clanging off in the distance, Polly would arrive and plunk Jefferson down on the quilt. She was only too glad to rush away, which was good, since Henry-James arrived shortly thereafter, out of breath with hurry and excitement. While he wolfed down his own can of dinner and much of the biscuits and strawberries and peppermint cakes the children brought in the basket, he devoured the lessons with his eyes.

When Jefferson formed words with the blocks, Henry-James ran his fingers over them.

When Jefferson called out the words on the cards, Henry-James mouthed them along with him.

When Jefferson chirped out the sentences in his little paper chapbooks about the greedy little boy being turned into a pig as punishment and the gossipy little girl waking up as a magpie, Henry-James was right there at his elbow, his face springing to life every time he saw a word he recognized.

When Jefferson got bored with the cards, Charlotte and Austin made more. This time they used words like *Rice, Hoe, Ash Cake,* and *Grits.* Henry-James was pleased with those.

When Jefferson grew tired of the chapbooks, Charlotte brought the *Charleston Mercury,* which was delivered to the plantation. Henry-James loved it when there were articles about Abraham Lincoln, the tall, homely Illinois lawyer some people wanted for President.

"Maximillian and I are tired of reading," Jefferson said one day. He kicked sullenly at the quilt. "We want to play."

"Who's Maximillian?" Charlotte said.

Austin rolled his eyes. "That's his imaginary friend."

"But he's real," Jefferson put in at once. He looked hard at Austin. "Even though I can't see him or touch him, I can hear him."

"Jus' like Jesus," Henry-James said.

Austin cocked his head. "Oh," he said. "I guess it is kind of like that."

"Except Jesus really was here at one time," Charlotte said. "You know—because the Bible tells us."

"And Daddy 'Lias," Jefferson said. "I want to go to Daddy Elias's and hear some more Jesus stories."

Austin had to admit he'd like to do that, too. Nobody could make Jesus seem real like Daddy Elias. All of this talk did give him an idea.

"Daddy Elias has to work," Austin told him. "But tomorrow we could *play* Jesus—and that might be almost as good."

Henry-James's brow went into rows deep as rice trenches. "What about my . . . what about them readin' lessons?" he said.

"Not to worry," Austin said.

The next day, a Bible was packed in the picnic basket with the ham biscuits and pickled peaches.

"What a wonderful idea," Sally Hutchinson said when Austin borrowed it from her. "Henry-James should like this."

"It isn't just for Henry-James," Jefferson piped up from the corner, where he was trying to figure out a Jacob's Ladder. "It's for me, and Charlotte, too. And Maximillian."

Mother arched her eyebrows at Austin. "Charlotte?" she said quietly.

"She's helping me teach Jefferson to read better," Austin said. He couldn't avoid her eyes.

She surveyed him for a moment, and then nodded. "And Henry-James is 'observing'," she said.

Austin ran his finger over the printing on the front of the Bible. "It wouldn't be Charlotte's fault if Henry-James learned something."

"You're taking a very big chance, Austin," she said. "I think you'd better talk this one over with Jesus. Didn't we decide that's what we were going to do from now on?"

But the Jesus game was such a huge success that there didn't seem to be any reason to ask Jesus if it was all right.

Every day Austin read a Jesus story out loud from the Bible, and he would stop now and then to point to a word and ask Jefferson what it was—with Henry-James watching carefully over his shoulder. Jefferson only stood for that exercise because he knew a game was coming.

When the story was read, they began acting it out.

One day they all came to Jesus-played-by-Austin with their crippled and maimed bodies and were healed.

Another day they watched in awe as Jesus-played-by-Jefferson multiplied the ham biscuits and fried chicken legs to feed his flock of thousands—played by three.

But it was the day that Jesus-played-by-Henry-James was teaching the four disciples the Lord's Prayer that something wonderful happened.

They were sitting in a circle, solemnly repeating the prayer after Henry-James. Austin imagined himself in a bed-sheet robe and sandals, sitting next to the bearded Jesus in awe and reverence. But as Henry-James finished the prayer in his rich, almost-manly voice and a silence settled over the group, the feeling that they were only playing went away.

It's real, he thought with a start. *This is as real as if Jesus were right here with us!*

He opened his eyes. Even though he saw only Henry-James, Charlotte, and Jefferson, that feeling *didn't* go away.

"I think Jesus is with us," he whispered.

No one laughed. No one rolled his or her eyes. They only nodded, even Jefferson.

"Just like Maximillian is," he said.

"Right," said Austin. "Only better."

Henry-James gave a decided nod. "Get them blocks, Massa Austin," he said. "I wants to make that word—*Jesus.* I wants to see what it look like."

Austin pulled the blocks out of the basket and spread them on the blanket.

"Find the J," he said.

Before anyone thought about it, Henry-James pawed

through the pile and produced the J. He mouthed the letter and looked at Austin.

"Next one gonna be E," he said.

Austin felt his face break into a grin.

"Good, Henry-James!" Charlotte cried.

"Z next?" Henry-James said when he'd added the E.

"No—S," said Jefferson. "That's a hard one."

Henry-James located the S and put it proudly into place. "Uh," he said. His brow wrinkled. "U?"

There was a round of clapping as Henry-James put the U and then another S in line on the quilt. Then he sat back and gazed at it in wonder.

"So that be what Jesus look like in words," he said in awe.

They all looked at it reverently, and Austin once again felt their friend among them.

And then he heard something—a sound none of them made. A rustling of bushes and the noise of footsteps padding away.

And silk rustling off down the path.

harlotte's face grew so pale that her freckles stood out like pepper flakes on mashed potatoes.

"Was that someone watching us?" she whispered.

"It must have been," Austin said. He dashed toward the hedge that separated them from the gardens and peered through, but saw no one.

"I know who it was," Jefferson said matter-of-factly. "That rustle-rustle sound—that's Polly's skirts. I hear it every time she chases me." He grinned devilishly. "And that's a lot."

Henry-James grew wild-eyed. "You got to go after her, Massa Austin," he said. "'Fore she tell her mama that Miss Lottie—"

"Don't worry," Austin said, scrambling for the picnic basket. "We're halfway there already."

But by the time they ran in through the back door of the Big House and down the hall, Polly's high-pitched voice was already whining out of the drawing room. They pushed Jefferson upstairs to go see his mother and then crouched

49

beneath the steps to listen.

"Is Charlotte allowed to play with that Henry-James?" Polly was saying. "I thought Daddy told her not to last winter."

"He did," Aunt Olivia said in a disappointed voice. "But he changed his mind after little Mr. Know-It-All Hutchinson talked to him. Why?"

Polly's tone drooped. "I just saw them down by the river, sitting on a quilt—all of them."

"She wouldn't be if I had my way," said Aunt Olivia with a loud sniff. "Wasting her time with both of those boys is why it becomes more and more hopeless that Charlotte will ever become a lady."

"She's wasting her time all right," Polly said. "They were playing with alphabet blocks. Can you imagine?"

There was a sudden silence. Austin looked fearfully at Charlotte.

"All three of them?" Aunt Olivia said slowly.

"Yes. Charlotte, Boston Austin, and Henry-James."

"*He*—that *slave boy*—was playing with *alphabet blocks?*"

"Yes!" Polly said—a little impatiently. "If she were playing at entertaining beaus or pouring tea, that would be one thing—"

"Polly, go and fetch your father," Aunt Olivia said abruptly. "And see if you can find Charlotte as well."

"Why?" Polly said. "I thought you said—"

"Just go, girl!" Aunt Olivia cried.

"Go" is what Charlotte and Austin tried to do—swiftly—before the drawing room door could open. But Polly spotted them from the doorway and shrieked, "Char-*lotte! Mama* wants to see you!"

Her howl brought the library door open, and Uncle Drayton appeared, his hair on end and his sleeves rolled up.

"What *is* it, Polly?" he said. "Can't a man have enough peace for a thought in this house?"

Polly could only point to where Charlotte and Austin were frozen in front of the back door.

"I see them," Uncle Drayton said irritably. "Unless they have committed a murder, I wish you would hush about them."

"They've done something almost as bad, I think," said Aunt Olivia from the drawing room doorway. "I must speak with you, Drayton, and I think Charlotte should be there, too."

Uncle Drayton sighed heavily. "All right, then, everyone in here. Come on, Austin. You, too."

Uncle Drayton managed to settle down Aunt Olivia enough to get her into a chair in his book-lined library. He motioned for Charlotte and Austin to sit on the green brocade settee, and he himself leaned against his big mahogany desk. This was a room Austin had spent many hours in, exploring Uncle Drayton's 200 volumes on dreary winter days. But right now he'd rather be anywhere else.

I wish Mother were down here, he thought desperately as he felt Charlotte quivering beside him. *She'd know what I was supposed to say now.*

"And Polly said they were playing with *alphabet blocks,*" Aunt Olivia was saying breathlessly to Uncle Drayton. "Now what reason could they have for doing such a thing other than to be teaching that slave how to *read?*"

She gave a self-righteous nod that set her double chin to wobbling. Uncle Drayton narrowed his eyes at Charlotte.

"Well, sweet thing?" Uncle Drayton said.

His use of his pet nickname for Charlotte did nothing to take the terror out of Austin's heart. He'd seen Uncle Drayton change from loving to irate in a matter of seconds.

"Were you indeed teaching that slave boy to read?" he said.

Charlotte's mouth opened, but nothing came out.

"Oh, for heaven's sake, girl, answer your father!" Aunt Olivia said. "I'd think you would have learned how to speak, as much time as you spend with this magpie!"

"May I answer that, sir?" Austin said.

"You see?" said Aunt Olivia.

Uncle Drayton shushed her with his hand and looked intently at Austin. For a rare moment, Austin was without words.

"First we can't shut him up," Aunt Olivia said. "Now he can't speak."

Time to be a magpie, Austin thought desperately. He took a big breath. "We were playing with alphabet blocks, all right!" he burst out. "That Jefferson, he's a Hutchinson for sure. I mean, I know he's becoming a fine horseman like the Ravenals—but he has the Hutchinson thirst for knowledge, you know? He wants to read, read, read—even during our dinnertime! We thought we might put him off a bit by bringing the blocks out—give us all a break from the constant study—"

"So it's Jefferson you're teaching to read," Uncle Drayton said.

"We're certainly helping Jefferson improve his skill, yes, sir," Austin said—truthfully.

"And this has nothing to do with—"

"Of course, Henry-James is there because, this time of year, what with the cottonmouths coming out, we need some protection. I've never seen a cottonmouth myself, of course, so what good would I be should one suddenly appear? I mean, I've *read* that they have a thick body and a whitish mouth—hence the name, I suppose—how clever—but I wouldn't know one if it dropped out of a tree. Although I've also learned that they will, on occasion, do just that very thing—"

"All right," Uncle Drayton said tightly. "I have no doubt that reading lessons are a form of sheer delight for you, Austin. Now, would you mind allowing Charlotte to answer for herself?" He turned to Charlotte. "Do you confirm all of this?" he said, not adding the "sweet thing."

"Yes, sir," Charlotte said faintly.

But that wasn't enough for Uncle Drayton. He stood for so long, arms crossed and eyes narrowed, that even Aunt Olivia began to rearrange her ruffles.

"I have only your word on it," he said finally. "I would like to think I can count on that." He stood up from the desk and circled around to the other side. He shuffled for a moment through the papers scattered there and ran his hand through his hair.

"The life you have always known, I fear, is about to change, Charlotte," he said. "Ever since that Stowe woman wrote that book—what is it, *Uncle Tom's Cabin?*—ever since then, the North has been determined to force us to give up slavery. Because of that, I must—" He suddenly stopped and scowled. "Why must I explain all this to you? I forbid you to teach a slave to read. That is the law, and it is final. Now go—both of you. I have things to do."

They both scrambled from the settee.

"I will be watching," he said as they hurried out the door.

"He'll have someone watching Henry-James like a hawk now," Charlotte said when they were safely outside again. She sank down under an oak tree. "I don't know how much longer we can get away with it."

Austin frowned at the palms of his hands. "I have to until Henry-James can read on his own. And then no one will be able to take that away from him—not ever." He looked at Charlotte. "But if you don't want to help anymore—"

"You're not leaving me out," she said. "We just have to be careful, that's all."

So they changed their plan a little. There were no more alphabet blocks or word cards or even chapbooks. The Bible and the Jesus game seemed the only safe way to go. And even that almost got them into the worst trouble yet.

It was the next Sunday, at St. Paul's Church. The slaves, as always, were tucked into the galleries while the white folks took the seats below. When the organ played to signal the first hymn, the lower congregation took up their hymnbooks and began to follow the words and sing. Above them, the blacks could only hum and sway and clap and insert their hallelujahs that to Austin were better than the regular words. He swayed a little himself as he sang along in his two-notes-flat voice.

What a friend we have in Jesus,
All our sins and griefs to bear.

Our friend, Austin said to himself. His mother had told him to work it out with that friend. It seemed like that was happening. He couldn't resist glancing up at Henry-James. When he did, his mouth stopped singing and fell open.

Henry-James was leaning over the railing, peering intently into the hymnbook of a tall man just below him. And he was singing as he read the words.

All because we do not carry—

Austin choked.

"Good heavens," whispered a voice two people down.

Austin flinched and tore his eyes away from Henry-James. But as he rested them on Uncle Drayton, he saw that he was looking right at the slave boy—and seeing it all.

Austin heard nothing of Reverend Pullens's sermon or the conversation inside the carriage as he rode home up front. All he could think about was the grave look on Uncle Drayton's face as he watched Henry-James openly reading a hymnbook.

I have to get to him before he gets to Charlotte, he thought.

He tried to feel Jesus there, the way he had that day when they were playing the game. He'd know just what to say.

But all Austin could think of were lies. Tell Uncle Drayton they'd sung the hymn for Henry-James so many times he'd memorized it. Convince him Henry-James had a gift for lip-reading. None of it seemed to be coming from Jesus.

As soon as they got home and Uncle Drayton flung open the front door, he said, "Charlotte Anne, I want to see you in my library—without your extra mouth." He bored his eyes into Austin and stomped off for the library. He stopped at the doorway and added tersely, "Everyone else—upstairs!"

As the skirts swished their way up the steps, Charlotte looked back at Austin helplessly.

What is this all about? her eyes said.

Austin could only shake his head. The lump in his throat wouldn't even let him answer.

Charlotte followed her father meekly toward the library like a lamb. He waited impatiently in the doorway for her to enter and gave Austin one last wilting look.

"Upstairs, Austin!" he barked. "At once!"

Austin turned toward the staircase with his heart pounding against his ears. He had taken only two steps when a shrill cry sliced the air from the landing above.

"Mama!" Polly shrieked. "Look what I've found—right in the middle of Kady's bed!"

Aunt Olivia's voice joined Polly's in a duet of screeching. Austin covered his ears and continued up, only to be bumped out of the way by a series of hoopskirts all vying to get to the bottom first.

"Your father will hear about this!"

"That is my private property!"

"You left it lying right out in the open!"

"In my room!"

"You had no business having it in the first place!"

Austin watched, open-mouthed, from the foot of the stairs as Aunt Olivia, Polly, and Kady squawked into each other's faces like angry birds in the hall. The library door flew open, and Uncle Drayton strode out with his arms stiff at his sides.

"What in heaven's name!" he trumpeted over them. "Quiet now! All of you!"

An unwilling silence fell over the group.

"Suppose you tell me what is going on here—one at a time!"

Austin saw Charlotte peeking timidly out the library door behind her father. Her face was still pale, but she didn't look as if she and Uncle Drayton had gotten far into their conversation. Her eyes found Austin's, and she raised her eyebrows in question.

"Polly," Uncle Drayton said sternly. "What is it you've found that is worth raising such a ruckus?"

"That, Daddy," she said, pointing her chin toward Aunt Olivia's hand.

Austin craned his neck to see. It was a book, and Aunt Olivia was holding it as if it might open its jaws at any moment and bite her.

Uncle Drayton sighed in exasperation. "Must we be so dramatic? What is it, Olivia?"

"It is a piece of northern filth!" Aunt Olivia cried.

"Let me see it."

Aunt Olivia punched the book toward him. Austin was sure he caught a gleam in her dark eyes, as if she'd just won a long, bitter argument.

Uncle Drayton sighed again and took the book from her. The impatience drained from his face as he looked at it, and the steely glint of anger took its place. He shot his eyes at Kady.

"Does this belong to you, Kady?" he said.

"It does now," Kady said calmly.

"Where did you get it?"

"Do you even have to ask?" said Aunt Olivia. "Sally Hutchinson gave it to her, as sure as I am standing here. Drayton, I have told you repeatedly—"

"Is that true?" Uncle Drayton said sharply to Kady.

"Yes," she said.

"Have you read it?"

"Most of it."

"Then you are aware that it is full of lies designed to cast the South in the worst possible light."

Kady shook her head, never taking her eyes from her father's. "It rings true as far as I can see," she said.

Uncle Drayton flipped the book open. Only then did Austin catch a glimpse of its cover. It read, *Uncle Tom's Cabin*.

Uncle Drayton thumbed the pages, his eyes taking in the words in fits and starts and his tongue sputtering as he read aloud.

""Well, Tom," said Legree, walking up and seizing him grimly by the collar of his coat, "do you know I've made up my mind to kill you? . . . Speak!" thundered Legree, striking him furiously. . . . And Legree, foaming with rage, smote his victim to the ground.""

Uncle Drayton looked up from the book with rage in *his* eyes. "Is that the way I treat my slaves, Kady?"

"The attitude is the same, Daddy. You think of them as pieces of property with no souls and no feelings—"

"I will not have my beliefs twisted about and thrown into my face like so much garbage, Kady Sarah!" Uncle Drayton's face was nearly purple, and his eyes were ablaze. Austin found himself shrinking away from the stair railing. "I have allowed you to explore your own ideas thus far because I thought it harmless. I thought your head would soon turn to thoughts of marriage and children and you would give up this nonsense."

"And she would have if it weren't for your sister!" Aunt Olivia put in.

"I am afraid at long last I must agree with you," Uncle Drayton said. "From this moment forward, you are to refrain from any more visits with your aunt." His voice crackled. "Return all reading materials you have taken from her and confine yourself to your room during your free hours."

Kady glared. "Until when?"

"Until I decide you will come out!" he said. "I am still the master of this house as well as this plantation—and I want every one of you to hear me!"

He circled his livid gaze around the hall, and even Polly cringed in its glare. When every head had nodded, he turned on his heel.

"Charlotte, you get on now," he said tightly.

Charlotte didn't need a second invitation to skitter out of the library and leave its slamming door behind her. She joined Austin on the stairway, where a tearful Kady had just passed on her run to her room. Aunt Olivia disappeared into the drawing room with Polly, and behind the door they could hear them whining in low voices. Above them, another door slammed—so hard it made the windows rattle.

✛ ✛ ✛

Chapter Seven

he family tomb is more cheerful than this house, Austin thought several times over the next few days. He wished someone would yell or scream at somebody, just to break up the solid silence.

Kady never emerged from her room except to give Charlotte and Austin their lessons, and even then she only pointed to a page in the primer or the arithmetic and then commenced to staring out across the rice fields at the slaves. Even at mealtimes she hurried upstairs to eat alone.

And Austin's mother behaved as if someone had died. She sighed a lot and seldom came downstairs, even to catch a sunny day in the cheerful drawing room.

One evening after supper when he was reading to her from the Bible, Austin looked up to find her gazing into the fireplace with a glaze thick as cake icing over her eyes. It was the third time that week it had happened.

Austin wiggled his eyebrows at the page of Matthew in front of him.

"'Then came Peter to him,'" Austin read aloud, "'and said, "Lord how oft shall my brother sin against me, and I forgive him? Till seven times?" Jesus saith unto him—'" Austin glanced at his mother "—nine thousand, five hundred forty-two divided by thirty-six."

Sally nodded vaguely at the fire, and then she shifted her eyes to Austin. "What was that last line?" she said.

"Long division," Austin said, slapping the Bible closed on his lap. "You aren't anywhere close to Galilee, Mother."

"I'm sorry," she said. She curled her thin fingers around her teacup and looked sadly into it. "I guess I'm too stuck on the problems of Canaan Grove to think much about anything else."

"You miss Kady?" Austin said.

"I miss Kady, I'm angry with Aunt Olivia, I'm *incensed* with your Uncle Drayton."

"That means you're double angry."

Mother set her teacup noisily into its saucer. "It means I'm so angry I could just . . . spit. He's my brother, but I want to throttle him."

Austin sat up straight in the brocade wing chair. "I don't think I like him anymore either. I used to want to be just like him, but you're right, I can't stand him anymore!"

He felt a rush of energy that made him cross his arms righteously over his chest and top it off with a nod. But Mother was shaking her head firmly.

"I didn't say I hated him, Austin," she said. "I love him so much—I could just shake him!"

"That doesn't make any sense," Austin said. "I don't think I'll ever forgive him for this."

The almost-see-through skin on his mother's forehead

wrinkled with worry. "Austin," she said, "what if I refused to forgive you for every mistake you've ever made? You would be locked in your room until you turned 18!"

"But this is different," Austin said. "I never did anything bad on purpose! This is worse than anything I've ever done!"

"It's the worst sins that need the most forgiveness," she said. And then she began to cough, and Austin had to get her water and rub her back. By the time she could breathe easily again, she was too tired to talk anymore.

The only person who seemed happy in the household was Aunt Olivia. She swished her silk skirts around looking quite smug about her accomplishment. But even that was squelched one Monday at the dinner table.

Everyone was picking at their chicken and corn pudding in suffocating silence when Aunt Olivia cut into it brightly.

"I miss Kady being here with us," she said.

Uncle Drayton grunted.

"I wish for all the world that she were sitting here beside me, tormenting Polly across the table," she went on.

Uncle Drayton looked up sharply from his plate. "You wanted her punished."

"I did not necessarily want *her* punished," Aunt Olivia said. "I just wanted that . . . *situation* . . . to come to an end."

"It's ended," Uncle Drayton said brusquely. He returned to his corn pudding. "That's that."

"I don't think it *is!*" Aunt Olivia said with alarm. "There is one more step you have yet to take, Drayton."

He didn't answer. Austin looked at Charlotte. She was staring a hole in her plate. Even Polly began to squirm.

"Did you hear what I said?" Aunt Olivia prodded.

"I did."

There was a jagged pause.

"Well?" she said. "What more evidence do you need that this arrangement is not working?"

"What arrangement?" Polly asked. "What do you mean?" Her bird hands were clenching the tablecloth.

"I *mean* it is unsatisfactory for Sally and her children to live under the same roof with us."

Austin's fork clattered to his plate. Next to him, Polly's neck seemed to stiffen right up out of her collar.

"You didn't tell me that!" she wailed. "You said if I brought you something about Kady and Aunt Sally, I would be helping Kady. You never said you were going to throw *them* out!" She glanced wildly at Austin. "She didn't tell me that, I swear!"

Austin stared first at her and then at Aunt Olivia, whose eyes were darting anxiously at her husband.

"I am not suggesting that we throw them out," she said. "But I think it is plain—"

Uncle Drayton cut her off with a roar. "You were using Polly and Kady to conspire against my sister?"

"Drayton, I was only doing what I thought best—"

"Oh, cease this!"

Silence descended on the room, except for the startled chattering of china from Uncle Drayton pounding his fist on the table.

"When was I replaced as the master of this house?" he shouted. The stabbing edge on his stare made Austin cringe. All eyes lowered to their plates as Uncle Drayton drew in an angry breath.

"I refuse to explain myself. I expect my word to be honored. Period. And I expect Kady to take her punishment for disobeying me." His gaze shot to Charlotte. "Just as I do all of my children. One scrap of evidence that that slave boy has been taught to read and you can expect the same."

Charlotte nodded her head as if the rest of her body were frozen. Austin found himself clinging to the sides of his chair.

"As for my sister and her boys," Uncle Drayton continued tightly, "I have no intention of tossing them out into the street. I have made no other arrangements for them at this time, and I will not be questioned about it again! Do I make myself clear?"

"Yes, Drayton," Aunt Olivia murmured.

Everyone else nodded soberly, and Uncle Drayton left the table with another rattling of crockery.

From then on, even Aunt Olivia and Polly tiptoed around the Big House as if stepping too hard would bring the roof crashing down.

But Austin didn't tiptoe. He marched around with his lips pressed tight and a rush of energy constantly pounding in his head.

Maybe Mother can still love Uncle Drayton—and Aunt Olivia and Polly—but I don't see how. If something like this happened to Charlotte and Henry-James, I'd never forgive him. Never.

The energy of anger was like steam, keeping him hard at the job at hand.

"Where is Jefferson?" he said one day on the quilt when Kady had silently collected her pens and books and gone back to the Big House. "Henry-James will be here soon, and we need to get on with the lessons."

Charlotte wrapped her checked apron around her finger. "Austin, what if—?" She stopped and wrapped the apron tighter.

"What if what?" Austin said.

"What if Daddy catches me?"

"You were the one who wanted to help. Quit if you want to, but I'm keeping on."

Charlotte pulled her eyebrows together. "That was mean," she said.

It didn't feel mean to Austin as he stiffened his shoulders. It felt . . . strong.

There was a stirring in the bushes, and Austin held up a warning hand. "Shhh, here they come," he whispered. "Are you still with me or not?"

Charlotte didn't answer. She just wrapped the apron tighter.

To Austin's surprise, it wasn't just Jefferson who came through the shrubs, but Polly, too. As Jefferson squirmed away from her, Polly stood rigidly at the edge of the quilt.

"I brought him," she said.

Austin felt the energy fill his chest. "So?"

"I just wanted you to notice that I'm keeping my promise."

"Do you want an award?" Austin said. "Shall we all clap for you?"

Polly's hands went to her skinny hips. "You're getting pretty high and mighty all of a sudden, Mr. Boston Austin," she said. "I was just going to say I was sorry—about Kady and all that." She tossed her head. "But now I'm not."

"Of course you're not," Austin said. "You don't know how to be sorry."

With that, Polly tried to bounce her lame curls again and stomped off through the shrubbery. Austin watched her with satisfaction. When he turned back around, Henry-James was hesitating at the other edge of the quilt.

"Come on, Henry-James," Austin said, waving his arm.

"There's no need to be afraid of her."

Henry-James nodded warily as he squatted on the quilt. "She did help us once," he said.

"That doesn't mean we should trust her," Austin said.

"Why is everybody different now?"

They all turned to look at Jefferson. He blinked his blue eyes back at them.

"Uncle Drayton doesn't take me out riding anymore. Nobody laughs. Polly doesn't even call me Brat." He scowled fiercely. "The only person who smiles is Maximillian."

"Too bad we can't see him," Charlotte muttered.

"Don't have to see him," Jefferson said. "I just know he's smiling. When are we going to play?"

"Now," Austin said, nodding his head decidedly. He looked straight at Charlotte. "If everybody is ready."

She looked back, but there was no friendship twinkle in her brown eyes, no we're-in-this-together shine. She searched his face for a moment, and then she took her eyes away as if she hadn't liked what she'd seen there.

For just a second, Austin's energy faltered. *What if she* doesn't *want to do this anymore? What if she's right—what if it's too dangerous?*

But the pounding in his head drummed that right out of his thoughts. *No. What I'm doing is right, and Uncle Drayton is wrong! I have to do this—Lottie or no Lottie.*

He pulled a newspaper out of the picnic basket.

"No!" Jefferson said noisily. "I want to play the Jesus game!"

"It doesn't matter what you want," Austin said. "I'm the teacher. Now come on. Try to read it."

But Jefferson crossed his chubby arms over his chest.

"No," he said. "I want to play the Jesus game."

"Read, shrimp!" Austin said through his teeth.

"Well, somebody do *some*thin'," Henry-James said. "Or that rice gonna be planted—with nothin' to show for it."

"All right," Austin said, head pounding. *"I'll* read."

Henry-James took his squatting position behind Austin, where he could peer over his shoulder. Jefferson crossed the quilt and plopped with a sulk into Charlotte's lap. Austin straightened his shoulders and began to read.

When he was finished, Henry-James rocked back on his heels. "What all of that mean?" he said.

Austin rattled the newspaper importantly. "It means the Democratic party tried to nominate a person to run for president," he said. "Only something went wrong and the men from the South got mad and went off to form their own party. They don't want a president who will take away the right to have slaves."

"Who gonna do that?"

"Abraham Lincoln would, if the Republicans nominate him," Austin said.

"Then that's who I wants for president," Henry-James said. And then he shrugged. "'Cept don't nobody care what I thinks."

"But someday they will," Austin said. He looked at Charlotte. "If Jefferson keeps getting better at reading."

Henry-James showed the space between his teeth in a half smile. Charlotte lifted her head and looked back at Austin.

"All right," she said in a voice he could barely hear. "As long as we're careful."

"And as long as we play the Jesus game next time!"

Jefferson said. "Or I'm not learning another thing!"

There was a burst of laughter, and for a moment the pounding stopped in Austin's head. *I knew it would be all right*, he thought. *I knew it would.*

The silence in the Big House, though, still seemed to be hanging as heavy as the draperies that afternoon when Charlotte and Austin came in the back hall to return the *Mercury* to the library. It was quiet, that is, until they heard the voices from inside.

"They've gone and made a mess of it!" Uncle Drayton was raving. "That's why I have to do it!"

"I'm sure those men know what they're doing—Robert Rhett and the rest!" Aunt Olivia said. "Why can't you just follow their lead?"

"Because I think they are leading us into trouble! I'd hoped the Democratic party could agree on a candidate, but the Southrons had to throw a fit and walk out. *Jefferson* would have acted better!"

"So they behaved poorly. What difference does it make?"

There was the sound of a fist pounding on desktop, and Austin and Charlotte jumped under the stairs.

"It makes a great deal of difference!" Uncle Drayton cried. "It means our leaders here in the South are bent on splitting the Union apart. They *want* to separate from the nation. They *want* a war—and I don't want that at all!"

"Neither do I, of course," Aunt Olivia said, her voice suddenly silky. "But what good will writing to Wesley Hutchinson do?"

Austin straightened, banging his head on the underside of the stairs. "Father?" he whispered.

"Wesley may be outspoken and obnoxious, but he is a brilliant man," Uncle Drayton said. "And he wants the nation held together as much as I do. I think perhaps he can tell me what is in the minds of the Northerners, something that might help me convince these southern hotheads to back away from this reckless path they're heading down."

"Reckless!" Aunt Olivia said. She tittered a rehearsed-sounding laugh. "These are men we've known all our lives, Drayton. You've always trusted them to make good decisions. Why not go along with them? You're going to stir up trouble, and we have enough suspicion cast on us now with this abolitionist woman living here!"

Her voice had wound up like a coil. Uncle Drayton pushed it down with another slap of his hand. Austin could almost see it descending on the desktop and his eyes driving Aunt Olivia back in her seat. His voice sounded like neither honey nor molasses.

"I am tired of going along with everyone else! My own daughter has pointed out that I never think a single issue through for myself. *Austin* takes more care in forming his opinions! And he is certainly more honest. Do you know that I have even taken to lying to protect my image as the infallible plantation owner?"

"Oh, Drayton, really—"

"Yes, really! I told the children Seton had been captured, just to prove I was right. I have no idea where he is—probably in Canada by now. It is time I gathered some information on my own and decided for myself what is right. This is no playful matter, Olivia. Everything about our lives may be lost if I do not act wisely."

"But contacting Wesley seems so rash—"

"I have already done it—and I will not discuss it further!"
She didn't answer.

"I am going to Charleston tomorrow," Uncle Drayton said
more quietly. "Should a reply arrive from Wesley while I'm
gone, you must have it sent to me immediately."

"This is dangerous, Drayton. You're bringing danger on
this house."

"Not half the danger there will be if I don't," he said.
"And don't you forget that."

Chapter Eight

"**S**o he's written to your father," Sally Hutchinson said.

Thoughtfully, she broke off a piece of tea cake from her tray and nibbled it. Austin selected one and cradled it in his hand—hoping a few crumbs would fall on Aunt Olivia's oriental rug.

"What do you think about that, Austin?" she said suddenly.

Austin stopped in midbite.

"You always think something," she said, smiling. "I thought maybe this had changed your mind a little about Uncle Drayton."

Austin felt his face cloud. It had at first. He'd crept out from under the stairs and dashed out the back door feeling a little taller inside than usual. Uncle Drayton consulting his father, admitting he himself might be wrong. . . .

But it was confusing. It stirred up doubts in his mind and kept that strong, sure energy from making things clear in there.

"He didn't say he'd let Kady come back and see you," Austin said. "Or let us teach Henry-James to read. He still believes in slavery."

"But he's trying, Austin," Mother said. "That's all Jesus expects of us."

"I don't care," Austin said. His head was starting to pound again. He sat up straight in the wing-backed chair and squared his narrow shoulders. "I still don't forgive him."

Mother put her morsel of tea cake back on the tray and watched him. Her honey-brown eyes drooped at the corners. They made Austin concentrate stubbornly on his next cake.

When she still kept watching, he set the cake down and picked up the Bible. "So, are we going to read tonight?"

Mother pushed a wisp of her hair off her forehead as if she were suddenly very tired. "I don't think it's doing much good," she said.

"It is!" Austin said. "Henry-James is learning to read this way!"

"But are *you* learning anything, Austin?" she said.

"I could read this backward," Austin said.

"But do you know what you're reading?"

Austin squirmed. He was feeling exasperated. "Of course I do!" he said.

"And do you practice it?"

"Can we just read?" Austin burst out.

Her face twitched. "Please don't use that tone with me, Austin," she said. "You never have. Don't start now."

Austin snapped the Bible closed. "Can I go now?"

"I think you'd better," she said.

She's wrong, his thoughts drummed at him as he marched across the hall to his own room. *Uncle Drayton is wrong and I'm right and that's all.*

Only the pounding of I'm-right energy kept him from running back to make up with his mother. And, besides, it seemed the next day that he *was,* indeed, right after all.

He and Charlotte and Jefferson were waiting for Henry-James as usual on the quilt when Bogie charged up the path. He threw his head back and howled, ears swaying joyously.

"He's trying to tell us something!" Austin said.

Even Charlotte smiled. "Where's Henry-James, Bogie?" she asked.

Bogie bayed happily again for an answer and then romped to the edge of the path and pointed his quivering nose. Henry-James appeared, grinning so broadly that the corners of his mouth nearly touched his earlobes.

"Did you get freed?" Jefferson said.

He did look *that* happy to Austin. "What is it? Tell us!" Austin said. "Bogie wouldn't!"

"Massa Austin, the rice done been planted," Henry-James said. He looked cautiously at Jefferson, still grinning. "And I think them snap beans is gonna sprout at the cabin tonight."

Austin's face split wide open. The pounding in his head quieted to a satisfied beat. *I was right. I was right.*

That night when Jefferson was safely snoozing into his pillow, Austin and Charlotte slipped with a bundle down the back stairs like a pair of shadows and flew across the plantation to Slave Street. Henry-James and Daddy Elias were waiting by the fireplace, faces glowing in the flicker of their tiny fire.

"Lordy, chilrun, I ain't never been so happy to see young'uns in my life," Daddy Elias said. "Henry-James got me curious as a coon."

Charlotte pulled a candle from the bundle and lit it in the fireplace. Austin pulled out the Bible.

"Now ain't this a treat?" Daddy Elias said, mouth going into its spoon-shaped smile. "You gon' read to us, Massa Austin?"

"Not me," Austin said. He grinned at Charlotte. Her brown eyes were dancing again.

"Oh," Daddy Elias said. His cloudy old eyes drooped—until Henry-James took the Bible from Austin and settled onto the worn rug at his grandpappy's feet. Lifting each page between his fingers as if he were handling a robin's eggs, he found his way to his place, his big lips silently forming words.

"Matthew, Chap—ter Eight—teen."

His eyes lit on the page like a pair of fireflies, and he spread his brown hands across the leaves and smoothed them down.

For a moment, he stared at the words as if they'd rearranged themselves since the last time he saw them. He darted his eyes up to Austin.

"You can do it," Austin whispered to him. "You know how."

Henry-James once again confronted the page. His lips opened and soundlessly formed a word.

And then he began to read—slowly, surely. "'There—fore is the kingdom of heaven like a cert—cert—like a king.'" He cleared his throat. "'For as much as the servant had not to pay, his lord co—mman—ded him to be sold, and his wife and chilrun, and payment to be made—'"

He stumbled more over the hard words, and Austin prompted him, "compassion" and "besought" and "tormentors."

But the last verse Henry-James struggled through by himself. "'So likewise shall my heavenly Father do also unto you, if ye from your hearts forgive not every one his brother.'"

When he was finished, the only sound was the satisfied slapping shut of the Bible. Charlotte beamed across the firelight at Austin, and he beamed back.

His head drummed softly. *I was right. I was right.*

"Lord, you done showed us a miracle here," Daddy Elias said. His frosty head was bowed and his eyelids were crinkled shut.

Austin knew he was praying in that way he had, as if he were just picking up on a conversation he'd been having with Jesus all day.

"Jesus," he went on, "You done taught this boy how to read Your Word. Seein' that, Lord—I can just go on to glory now."

The old man lifted his face to smile on his grandson. Henry-James tugged at Bogie's ear and shrugged.

"Was Massa Austin and Miss Lottie done taught me to read," he said. "You best thank them, too."

"Who's gónna thank them when you gets whupped clean to the bone?"

Austin jerked his head from the gleaming faces of Henry-James and Charlotte and Daddy Elias to a tall, dark silhouette in the cabin doorway. All Austin could see was the glint in Ria's eyes as she moved inside and closed the door behind her. The quiet in the room grew hard.

"Nobody gonna answer me?" she said. She went to the fire and began to poke it savagely. Startled sparks spat out at her.

"I wasn't plannin' on gettin' no whuppin', Mama," Henry-James said, staring down at the cover of the Bible. "Ain't nobody gonna find out."

"What makes you so sure of yourself, boy?"

Henry-James didn't answer. Charlotte was watching him

painfully, winding her apron around her finger, and Daddy Elias had his eyes closed.

Austin's head pounded. *"I'm* sure," he said. "Fast as Henry-James learned to read, he's surely smart enough to keep anybody from finding out."

Ria whirled from the fireplace. "And you don't think Marse Drayton just as smart?" she said, spitting out her words like the sparks behind her. "I saw him a-lookin' at Henry-James jus' the other Sunday in church while he was *readin'* the hymns plain as day—" She stopped and stabbed the fire poker into its holder. Slowly, she narrowed her eyes at Austin. "'Scuse me for sayin', Massa Austin," she said coldly, "but it seem to me that if Henry-James gets hisself caught knowin' how to read, *you* the one oughta get whupped for it."

Austin straightened his shoulders. "I'd take a whipping for Henry-James in a minute!"

Ria grunted. "I reckon that's easy for you to say, Masta Austin, seein' how Marse Drayton would never allow such a thing." She thrust a long finger toward him. "No, if'n Henry-James gets hisself caught, *he* the one gonna get whupped, *he* the one gonna get sold to Georgia for to die in a cotton field. And *you* gonna carry that on your head the rest of your life, 'cause I ain't never gonna forgive you."

"Mmmm-mmmm," Daddy Elias muttered from deep in his throat.

"Don't you be tellin' me what I should be thinkin', Daddy," Ria said to him. "It ain't gonna do you no good."

With that, she stepped through the doorway into the bedroom and yanked the curtain closed—so hard that the faded red cloth swayed in the silence she left behind her.

Austin looked helplessly at Charlotte, but her eyes had

shot straight to Daddy Elias.

"Don't you chilrun worry none about Ria," he said, his eyes still closed. "She'll have her a talk with Jesus. He'll set her straight." He rocked soothingly and smiled into his own mind. "We done seen us a miracle here tonight. S'posin' we rest our heads on that?"

Henry-James was still watching the curtain settle into stillness, but slowly his forehead smoothed out, and Austin saw the space between his two front teeth.

That's the happiest I've ever seen him look, Austin thought. *We did that—and we're going to make sure it stays that way.*

The spring rains began the next day and went on for three days. That was good for helping flood the fields of newly planted rice but boring for Charlotte and Austin, who had to have their lessons in the music room. While Austin and Charlotte yawned over their multiplication tables, Kady sat on the red sofa and gazed at the tracks the rain made down the windows. By the third day, Austin could recite every table sideways, and he found his thoughts hammering back to Kady. He went to the door and peeked out into the empty hall. Making sure the door was shut behind him, he went over to Kady.

"I think you should just do whatever you think is right, Kady," he whispered. "No matter what Uncle Drayton says."

She looked at him over a gray satin shoulder as if she'd only just noticed he was there.

"Oh, you do, do you?" she said.

"That's what Charlotte and I did," he said, keeping his voice low. "We didn't let Uncle Drayton make our decisions for us, right, Lottie?"

Charlotte looked up from her slate, but she didn't say anything. Her freckles stood out against her pale face.

"You could keep learning from my mother, and no one could take that away from you," Austin went on.

"I don't think so, Austin," Kady said.

"You think your father is wrong, don't you? Aren't you angry? Don't you just hate him sometimes?"

She gave him a long look. "I like the kinds of questions you used to ask better," she said.

Austin didn't have a chance to ask her what she meant. The door burst open, and Aunt Olivia swept in. Her double chin seemed to have tripled, and it was agitating excitedly over her lace collar.

Kady turned abruptly back to the window, and Charlotte buried her face in the nines tables. But Aunt Olivia turned her stormy eyes right on Austin.

"Thank heaven you're in here," she said. "I want you to go on an errand for me."

Austin blinked and looked around. "Me?"

"Yes, you! A message has arrived, and I need for you to accompany that slave boy—what's his name? Oh, you know, that Henry-James. I want you to go with him to Charleston and take the message to your uncle."

Austin stared at her blankly. "You want me to drive to Charleston?"

"Not drive. Don't be absurd. You'll take a pirogue up the river. It's ready for you by the rice mill. I've sent for the boy."

She was talking in chopped-up sentences, and Austin's head bobbed to keep up.

"What's a pirogue?" he said. "Doesn't Henry-James have work to do? Doesn't he have to tend the sluice gates now that they've been opened?"

"Any of the slaves can do that," Aunt Olivia said fretfully.

"Not really," Austin said. "I've read all about it. Each slave has certain tasks, and not just anyone—"

"You are the most annoying boy!" Aunt Olivia cried. "Just go to the rice mill and meet the boy! You should be in Charleston in no more than three hours. Mr. Ravenal is at the Mills House on Meeting Street."

"But how—?"

"It's a short walk from the dock." Aunt Olivia glanced out at the rain. "I doubt you'll melt."

"What message—?"

Aunt Olivia took him by the arm and steered him to the door. "The boy already has it. I wrapped it in tinfoil." She shook Austin slightly. "If anyone should stop you, do not tell them where you've come from."

Austin caught his breath. "Is this a secret message?"

"As if it were any of your business!" Aunt Olivia said. Her chins quivered, and she brought Austin's palm up and slapped a piece of paper into it. "Here is the boy's pass. Go straight to the boat now."

"I'll need to tell my mother," Austin said.

Aunt Olivia waved a plump hand impatiently. "I've already told her. Now go—and hurry!"

"But I still don't understand," Austin said. "Why am *I* to go?"

Aunt Olivia flapped her hands frantically in front of her face, rings gleaming. "Your father has created this wretched errand!" she cried. *"You* should be the one to go on it!"

✠ ✠ ✠

Chapter Nine

*A*ustin stared at her only a moment longer before she shoved past him out the music room door, spitting over her shoulder, "Go at once! Hurry!"

When she was gone, Austin's face split into a grin. "I'm going on an adventure!"

"Adventure my left shoe," Kady hissed, bustling to close the door. "It's a suicide mission!"

"I don't understand," Austin said.

"What if the dugout turns over? You can't swim."

"She said we're going in a pirogue."

"A pirogue *is* a dugout. You see what I mean? You're totally unprepared for this. I can't believe she's sending you."

Austin stood taller. "I suppose she thinks I'm the best person for the job, seeing how the message is from my father."

Kady opened her mouth, but she closed it again and took Austin by both shoulders. "Be careful, Austin," she said. Her deep-brown eyes were pools of concern. "Tell Henry-James to put the message in his mouth. If someone does stop you, they probably won't think to look there."

"Why would anyone stop us?"

"You've read the newspaper. You know how much squabbling is going on. If anyone finds out my father is receiving a message from an abolitionist, who knows what could happen to—"

"I'm sorry, Kady, but I don't much care what happens to Uncle Drayton now. Not after what he's done to you and all."

Kady squeezed his shoulders and let go. "Just be careful," she said. "And at least go upstairs and fetch a jacket. You can't go up the river in your shirtsleeves in this rain."

Austin nodded and hurriedly escaped into the hallway. He could hear Kady whispering to Charlotte as the door closed behind him.

I didn't even say good-bye to Charlotte, Austin thought as he took the steps two at a time. *I wish she were going with us. We never have adventures without Lottie.*

But when he was tucked into his corduroy cutaway and racing between the Monarch Lakes toward the rice mill in the rain, his heart began to sail, too. This wasn't just a game they'd be playing in some old split-out canoe on the bank, the way they had last winter. This was real—and he was being trusted to do it.

What's Kady worried about anyway? he thought. *Henry-James will be with me. He's probably done this a hundred times.*

The dugout was slanted on the riverbank when he got there, and Henry-James was just emerging from the rice mill with a paddle in one hand and a small wad of tinfoil in the other. His face was solemn, and Austin tried to match his to it, but he couldn't keep it from breaking into a grin so big that he could see his own cheeks poking out like apples under his eyes.

"What you grinnin' for, boy?" Henry-James said. "We goin' for a two-hour paddle in the rain, and you smilin' like you done got yourself a Christmas gift."

"I have!" Austin said. "You and I are being sent to Charleston—all by ourselves!"

Henry-James grunted, but Austin detected a tiny sparkle in his black eyes.

"So let's go!" Austin said. He headed toward the dugout, where a blanket bulged in the rear. "What's that?" he said.

"Josephine done packed us some food and blankets."

"Then what are we waiting for? Oh." Austin pointed to the tinfoil. "Kady says to carry that in your mouth."

Henry-James didn't even blink as he rolled the message into the tinfoil until it was toothpick-thin and stuck it in his mouth. It didn't even make a bulge in his cheek.

"This is important," Austin said, trying once more to look serious. But his face broke into a grin again. "Still, there isn't any reason we can't have fun, is there?"

Henry-James almost smiled, too. "At least you back, Massa Austin," he said.

"What do you mean, I'm back?"

"You been madder'n a sow what's got somebody tryin' to take her piggies here lately," he said. "'Bout time you got back to the old Massa Austin."

"I still don't know what you're talking about," Austin said. "Now, how do I get in this thing without turning it over and drowning us both?"

"*That's* what I's talkin' about," Henry-James said. And

this time he did smile.

It took only two tries and one dip into the river up to his knees for Austin to get himself settled in the dugout. Henry-James made him sit in the middle because the bundle Josephine had put in the rear of the boat weighed it down.

The rain was slowing down to a warm drizzle as Henry-James dipped his paddle into the Ashley River, first on one side of the canoe and then on the other, until Canaan Grove began to disappear behind the rain and the dripping Spanish moss.

Henry-James kept the boat as close to shore as he could, and Austin called out questions about the sights he saw along the bank.

"What's that church?"

"That there's St. James Goose Creek."

"Who lives in that house?"

"Them's the Singletons."

"And there?"

"Dr. Garden. They calls that house Otranto."

"I know a novel about that! It was a ghostly castle."

After that the shores turned into solid walls of trees, already thickening the woods with their spring buds. Then Austin thought up a game and wheedled Henry-James into playing it with him. By the time they reached the spot where the Ashley began to widen, Henry-James had admirably played the part of a Yamasee Indian warrior making friends with an English explorer. Between that and the paddling, he'd also worked up an appetite.

"Can we stop and have us a bite to eat, Massa Austin?" he said. "This here's a good time, what with the rain stoppin' for a while."

"What are you asking me for?" Austin said. "You're the one doing all the work!"

"'Cause you the white man," Henry-James said, "so you the boss."

"Not me," Austin said as Henry-James paddled the canoe neatly into a nook in the riverbank. "I don't believe in that. Besides, I've never done this before. You have."

Henry-James furrowed his forehead at him. "No, I ain't," he said. "I ain't never been to Charleston my whole life."

Austin felt his eyes spring open. "You haven't!" He cocked his head. "Then I wonder why Aunt Olivia—"

"Let's jus' have us somethin' to eat," Henry-James said. "Lemme get this here message out of my teeth."

He stuck his finger into his mouth and produced the tinfoil.

"How do you talk with that thing in there?" Austin said as he made his way carefully toward the blankets. "I knew it was small, but I forgot you even had it."

"I jus' don't talk as much as you does," Henry-James said dryly.

With his hand on the blanket, Austin looked back over his shoulder at Henry-James and grinned. "Isn't this the best day of your life so far, Henry-James?" Austin said. He gave the blanket a yank and watched Henry-James's eyes grow round and wide as a pair of Aunt Olivia's china dinner plates.

"What?" Austin said.

Henry-James could only point toward the bundle containing their lunch.

Austin turned to it and saw not a basket stuffed with corn-bread and pickled peaches but Charlotte, curled into a ball and soaking wet.

"Lottie!" Austin cried. "What are you—? How did you get

in—? No wonder the back end was so weighted down. I mean, not that you're heavy, but you're certainly heavier than a picnic supper. Does anyone know you're here?"

"You're right, Henry-James," Charlotte said as she uncurled herself and stretched. "The old Austin is back."

She grinned until her freckles danced in the wrinkles on her nose. But Henry-James didn't crack a smile.

"You done sneaked aboard this here dugout, Miss Lottie?" he said, forehead in double rows of furrows.

"Yes," Lottie said proudly. "Kady said I could come down and say good-bye, but neither one of you was there yet and here was this perfect blanket for me to hide under, so . . ."

She shrugged.

"Somebody might coulda caught you!" Henry-James said sternly.

"Certainly not you two!" she said. "You never even noticed that I was mighty big for a picnic."

Henry-James scowled, but Austin couldn't hold back another grin. "I was just *hoping* it was a supper that big!" he said. "I mean . . . but I'm glad it's you instead."

"You gonna be glad when her daddy find out she come with us?" Henry-James said.

"He'll never know," Charlotte said. "I'll stay hidden."

Henry-James grunted harshly.

"Please don't be mad at me, Henry-James," she said. To Austin's surprise, her brown eyes swam miserably. "I just didn't want to be left out!"

"You know," Austin said quickly, "when I was on the way down to the boat, I was thinking how I wished she would come along. It wouldn't be the same having an adventure without Lottie."

Henry-James examined a piece of batter cake smothered in apple butter and scowled at it.

"We're lucky to have a friend like her," Austin pushed on. "We could just have imaginary friends, like Jefferson does."

At that, Henry-James's lip twitched. "What's that boy's name? Max-i-millian?"

Charlotte giggled. "You don't have to see him or hear him—you just have to know he's there."

"And he's *way* bigger than me," Austin said.

They chattered on about Maximillian and about Polly's egg shells and beet juice and about the splendid look on Daddy Elias's face when he realized Henry-James was actually reading—and the anger of the past days all faded away. When they polished off the last of the batter cake and strawberries, they started off again down the river and pretended they were abolitionists about to set the cotton planters' slaves free.

But as the roofs of Charleston came into view, Henry-James sat straight up in the front of the canoe and said firmly, "Miss Lottie, now you get yourself under them blankets again, 'fore somebody sees you."

Charlotte obediently got out of sight, and Austin got up on his knees, questions tumbling out one on the heels of another.

"Is that the Citadel I've read about, where they train the soldiers? That looks like a rice mill, but it's much bigger than Uncle Drayton's. I didn't think anybody grew more rice than he does. Do they?"

"You askin' the wrong person, Massa Austin," Henry-James said. "I done tol' you, I ain't never been to Charleston."

And he looked as if he wished he were anywhere else

right now. The canoe was dwarfed by the tall, masted ships and schooners that lined the bank, and Henry-James's dark eyes were wide as he glanced warily at them and paddled with his head low as if he weren't supposed to be there at all.

"You all right, Lottie?" Austin whispered in the direction of the blankets.

"I'm fine," she hissed back. "Go to the dock at Tradd Street. You'll see the Chisholm Rice Mill. I know how to get to the hotel from there."

"See?" Austin said to Henry-James. "It's a good thing she came along."

Henry-James glowered at the docks and kept paddling. Austin's head swiveled like a duck's as he took it all in—the masts poking up in bunches along the wharves, their flags standing out like loosely starched, rippling rectangles . . . the gulls with their winged shoulders hunched up against the wind . . . the thick lines like braids holding the boats in place and creaking and flapping their tasseled ends in the breeze.

"Let's pretend we're taking you to Boston Harbor!" Austin said. "Let's pretend we're taking you to college there!"

But Henry-James ducked his head and pulled the dugout up against the dock at the rice mill. "Let's pretend we don't see them Patty Rollers standin' right up there," he muttered.

Austin craned his neck with a start. There were two men approaching the dock, arms pumping importantly at their sides. But Austin knew at once they weren't the men who patrolled the plantations, looking for slaves off their land without passes. At least they weren't Barnabas Brown and Irvin Ullmann, the Patty Rollers Austin knew. And in their brown wool frock coats and silk brocaded waistcoats, they were too well dressed to be out scavenging for slaves to get money from slave owners.

"Don't worry, those aren't Patty Rollers," Austin said. "And besides, I have a pass for you. We have every right to be here."

But Henry-James stiffened as the two men reached the dock and watched the boys climb from the dugout and pull it to a slant on the riverbank. Henry-James kept his head low as he tied the canoe off. Austin looked right up at them, shielding his eyes from the sun, which was now making its descent down the other side of the sky.

"Good afternoon," he said cheerfully.

The taller of the two men looked down at him from under a set of eyebrows that met in the middle.

"State your name, boy!" he said—not at all cheerfully.

Austin felt Henry-James shrinking into his shirt as he stepped behind him. The energy at once began to pound in Austin's head, and the playful ride down the river faded away like a dream.

"Why?" Austin said.

The short, stout man with side whiskers that met his mustache harrumphed loudly.

"I am not in the habit of explaining myself to insolent young boys!" he said.

And I am not in the habit of explaining myself to rude old men! Austin wanted to say. But behind him, Henry-James was tugging at his cutaway jacket. And in front of him, the two men were approaching with wrath in their eyes.

"Come up here, both of you," Eyebrows called.

Pretending to make his way up to the road by his own choice, Austin obeyed, with Henry-James close on his heels.

"What is your business here, now?" said Side-Whiskers,

snatching Austin roughly by the arm. For men who dressed like gentlemen, they acted like street ruffians, as far as Austin was concerned.

"I'm here to see my uncle," Austin said. He tried to pull his arm away, but Side-Whiskers held on tighter.

"And this is your boy?" Eyebrows said.

Austin winced, but he nodded. The two men's air wasn't that of the southern gentlemen Austin had met. They acted more like policemen who were questioning criminals. It drained the angry energy right out of Austin's head and put a jittery, clawing feeling in its place. Better just to answer the questions and be on their way.

"You have a pass for him, I assume," said Side-Whiskers, shaking Austin's arm.

"Are you Patty Rollers?" Austin said innocently.

"You insult me with your impudence!" Side-Whiskers cried. "Have you a pass or not?"

Austin nodded and reluctantly pulled the pass from the front pocket of his cutaway. It was damp from the rain and the splashing of the Yamasee Indian scene, but the ink of Aunt Olivia's handwriting was still legible.

Side-Whiskers took the pass, and Eyebrows read it over his shoulder. Austin thought hard to stop his heart from hammering.

We have nothing to be afraid of. We have a pass. We're not doing anything wrong. We're only going to see Uncle Drayton. We have nothing to hide—

Except Charlotte.

And the note in Henry-James's mouth.

"You're Drayton Ravenal's nephew?" Side-Whiskers barked.

"Yes," Austin said, trying to smile. "You know him, of course. He's quite well known in Charleston."

"I know him." Side-Whiskers gave Eyebrows a dark look. "Though not as well as I thought I did. Crying 'Save the Union' when the rest of us are ready to secede—"

But Eyebrows suddenly cut him off with his hand. "Hold on here!" he said. "He could be worse than Drayton Ravenal's nephew."

The tall man bent over Austin and pulled him up close to his face by the front of his cutaway. Austin could hear a low growl coming from Henry-James's throat.

"What's your name, boy?" Eyebrows said. "No more of your games. Who are you?"

"He said he was Ravenal's nephew," Side-Whiskers said.

"And don't you know who Ravenal's nephew is?" Eyebrows snapped at him. His brows tangled together in an angry knot. "If he's Ravenal's nephew, he's Wesley Hutchinson's son!"

Side-Whiskers yanked Austin away from Eyebrows with a jerk so hard that it rocked Austin's head on his neck.

"Are you a Hutchinson, boy?" he said. "Do you belong to that abolitionist animal?"

Although Austin's heart raced in his ears, he clamped his mouth shut.

There is no way they will know unless I tell them, he thought. *And they're never going to hear it from me!*

Not with Charlotte to protect—and Henry-James.

"Answer me, you insolent cur!" Side-Whiskers shouted into his face.

Austin squeezed his eyes shut. If they were going to hit him, he didn't want to see it.

A hand shoved his chest, and he fell backward against Henry-James. But the black boy was suddenly seized from behind him. Austin opened his eyes to see Eyebrows grab on to the back of Henry-James's shirt and rip it cruelly all the way down the middle.

"What are you doing?" Austin cried.

"We're searching your slave, boy!" Eyebrows said. "You're hiding something, and I bet I know where it is."

"Come here, you little cuffee!" Side-Whiskers said.

Eyebrows sent Henry-James flying toward his tall partner, who snatched him up by the neck with both hands.

"Open your mouth, darky!" he shouted. "Open your mouth and let me see what you're hiding for Wesley Hutchinson's son!"

Chapter Ten

Austin lunged forward, but Eyebrows grabbed him by the sleeve and held him while he flailed helplessly. Side-Whiskers pried open Henry-James's mouth and peered inside. Austin stopped struggling and held his breath.

"Open wider, you little beast!" the man cried. "You can't hide anything now!"

If Henry-James tried to open his mouth more, Austin couldn't tell. Side-Whiskers shoved at his upper teeth with the heel of his hand and the black boy's head jerked back.

"You're hurting him!" Austin shouted at him. But he knew this was nothing compared to what was going to happen when the man found that wad of tinfoil tucked behind Henry-James's molars.

Side-Whiskers ignored him as he scoured the inside of Henry-James's mouth with his eyes. Then he let go, and with a palm to Henry-James's chest he sent him teetering backward.

"Nothing!" Side-Whiskers said. His nostrils flared as if

92

Henry-James had insulted him by *not* trying to sneak something past him. Austin stared. Where had the message gone?

Eyebrows shook Austin by the back of his jacket. "Are you bringing Yankee information to your uncle?"

"Of course he is!" Side-Whiskers nearly screamed. "You heard Drayton Ravenal at that meeting this morning! He came right out and said he was going to reserve judgment until he had more information. What information does he need? He's lived here in the low country all his life!"

Eyebrows tightened his hold on Austin's jacket, pinching a hunk of skin with it. Austin bit back a yelp.

"Where is it?" he hissed in Austin's ear.

"He isn't going to tell you. You know those Yankees don't teach their chilrun any manners!" Side-Whiskers flared his nostrils wider. "The dugout. I'll check there."

Austin looked frantically at Henry-James, who was still lying on the ground. Henry-James watched the tall man pick his way back to the pirogue, but Austin couldn't look. Any second now, the man was going to rip the blanket back and expose Charlotte—and there was going to be no end to the trouble for all three of them. Austin started preparing a speech for his uncle in his mind.

"There's nothing here but a picnic basket and two blankets," Side-Whiskers called from the bank.

Austin's eyes locked with Henry-James's. He had to force himself not to look around for Charlotte. *Where could she have gone?* he wondered. There was no way she could have slipped past them.

"There's only one way to find out what Ravenal is up to with this," Eyebrows said as Side-Whiskers joined him. "We'll have to take these two to him and ask him outright."

Side-Whiskers tugged at the waistcoat that was pulled tightly across his belly and nodded. "You have rope in the carriage?"

"Yes."

"I'll get it. We'll have to tie up the slave."

Austin ripped his jacket away from Eyebrows. "Why?" he cried.

"I've never seen a darky yet who didn't take every chance available to run away," Eyebrows said as his partner moved off toward a plum-colored Dearborn carriage with a bay harnessed to it. The horse stomped nervously when Side-Whiskers drew near.

I don't blame her, Austin thought. *These men are evil!*

He was about to turn and tell Eyebrows there was no need to bind Henry-James when his eye caught on something under the dock. There was something behind one of its piers—and it was too big to be a gull.

Glancing quickly at Eyebrows to be sure he didn't see it, Austin peered harder. From behind the pier, a trail of deer-colored hair flew up in the wind and settled back down.

"All right, boy, get up," Side-Whiskers called out to Henry-James as he plodded toward them again. Although the rain had left the spring afternoon cool, the stout man was dripping sweat from his nose and huffing like a steam engine.

Austin lurched for him and grabbed the rope. "I'm responsible for Henry-James!" he cried. "As long as he's with me, he won't try to run away."

"Let go of that rope, you miserable mongrel!" Side-Whiskers shouted. "Turn it loose!"

Austin hung on and let the two men wrestle him for it. Side-Whiskers was too out of breath to be of much good, but

Eyebrows wrenched it away, burning Austin's hands in the process and wrapping it tightly across his chest.

"You're the one who should be tied up!" he growled into Austin's ear.

"Fine with me," Austin said. "But it isn't going to be fine with my uncle when he finds out."

"We're not afraid of that Yankee-lover!"

The two men went on tossing insults about Uncle Drayton back and forth as they shoved Austin and Henry-James back to back and coiled the rope around them from chest to thighs. It gave them enough to do that they didn't notice the little figure in the sopping-wet apron dashing from the dock to the Dearborn and slipping inside. Austin tried not to smile. The horse never even whinnied.

Tying up prisoners was obviously not something Eyebrows and Side-Whiskers did often, because once they had their captives attached so tightly they could hardly walk, they were hard put to figure out a way to get them to the carriage and inside.

They ended up toting them like a large sack of grain and shouting instructions and complaints at each other all the way. It gave Austin a chance to whisper to Henry-James.

"Message?"

"Swallowed it. Miss Lottie?"

"Carriage."

It was enough to make being dumped like cargo onto the floor of the carriage cab bearable. The two men slapped the door shut and climbed into the driver's seat above. Austin couldn't wait to hear what Uncle Drayton was going to say when he saw this scene.

He's also going to see how smart Henry-James is, and

how loyal, he thought as they bounced over the cobblestone street. *He's risked one walloping stomachache to keep his master out of trouble.*

"Hey, Miss Lottie," he heard Henry-James whisper behind him.

"Where is she?" Austin hissed.

"Under this here seat."

"We can almost touch noses!" Charlotte whispered across them.

In spite of the rope cutting into his jacket, Austin did smile then. This was turning out to be more of an adventure than he'd bargained for.

The Dearborn lurched to a stop, and through the carriage box's swinging curtains Austin could see a five-story building with an iron balcony on its second floor. He'd read about the Mills House Hotel in the *Mercury.* They'd called it the "largest and most commodious building in the city." It figured Uncle Drayton would stay there. If he wasn't going to open up the Ravenals' town house for just a few days, he was going to have to find his luxury somewhere.

The carriage door flew open, and Eyebrows reached in and caught Henry-James by the foot. He and Austin were hauled like a bundle out of the cab and dropped soundly onto the sidewalk. Henry-James was on the bottom, and Austin heard him groan.

"Now, how are we going to get them inside the hotel?" Side-Whiskers asked.

"Call a steward!" Eyebrows said, and then he gave a harsh laugh. "You stay here with the booty. I'll go in and fetch Ravenal."

For the first time since he'd spotted Charlotte under the

dock, Austin's heart sank. If they were going to bring Uncle Drayton out here, how was Charlotte going to get out of the carriage and out of her father's sight?

Maybe this wasn't such a good idea, Austin thought nervously. *Maybe she should have just gotten back in the dugout to wait for us.*

Underneath him, Henry-James moaned again, and Austin tried to wriggle them sideways. Side-Whiskers planted a foot on Austin's stomach.

"Don't try anything with me, boy," he said. "Any Yankee is as low as a slave as far as I'm concerned. I won't treat you any different."

Austin glared at him fiercely. Jeering through yellowed teeth, the man placed his foot firmly on the side of Austin's face and pushed it away.

Austin didn't move after that.

Around them, the wheels of carriages and buggies whirred and horses' hooves clopped and people's chatter turned to gasps as they passed the bundle of boys on the sidewalk. All of it was drowned out by the pounding of anger in Austin's head.

Wait until Uncle Drayton sees this! he kept thinking. *I hope he challenges them to a duel—both of them—right here on the spot!*

A trumpeting voice interrupted his vision.

"What in heaven's name is this?"

"They refused to cooperate," Side-Whiskers said. "We had no choice!"

Austin stretched his neck and saw Uncle Drayton staring down at him, his handsome chin jutted out in disbelief.

"Austin, what on earth!"

Austin opened his mouth—and promptly closed it again. He'd been so busy dreaming up Side-Whiskers's and Eyebrows's demise that he hadn't planned what he was going to tell Uncle Drayton in front of them. With any luck, his uncle wouldn't ask too many questions until they were gone.

"Is this your nephew, Ravenal?" Side-Whiskers barked.

"It is indeed. You untie him at once!"

"And your slave?"

Eyebrows rolled both of them with his foot. Drayton gazed down at Henry-James.

"You!" Uncle Drayton cried. "Austin, I demand an explanation."

So much for luck, Austin thought. He took a deep breath.

"It isn't his fault, Uncle Drayton," he said. "I wanted an adventure. I've been wanting one ever since I got here, so I ordered him to bring me to Charleston to see you."

"That is the lamest thing I've ever heard!" Side-Whiskers said. "If you expect us to believe that—"

"I'm afraid it's entirely true," Uncle Drayton said. His face went from angry to grim, and he leaned over and yanked at the rope. "He may be Wesley Hutchinson's son, but he has none of his brains, I can tell you that. This is exactly the kind of thing I have come to expect of him."

He dropped the loose rope on the sidewalk and pulled Austin up by the arm. He poked Henry-James—gently, Austin saw—with his toe.

"Get up, you," he said. He looked at Side-Whiskers. "Thank you for bringing them to me. I will deal with them now."

Austin stared, open-mouthed. He hadn't really expected a duel, but shouldn't these two at least get a good chewing out?

Eyebrows growled. "Once we have proof of your lack of loyalty to the South, Ravenal, you'll be run out of Charleston on a rail."

"Wait!" Side-Whiskers suddenly burst out. "We never searched the white boy!"

"Nor shall you!" Uncle Drayton trumpeted back at him.

Eyebrows and Side-Whiskers both leapt forward, hands groping for Austin. Uncle Drayton pushed Austin aside and hurled himself at the two men. As Austin stumbled across the sidewalk, he saw his uncle wrap his arms around Eyebrows's long legs and drop him to the ground, knocking Side-Whiskers down like a domino behind him.

The fat man's heavy body rolled into the road, where the startled bay whinnied in terror. She rose up on her back legs and took off at a frightened trot down Meeting Street, pulling the Dearborn behind her.

With Charlotte in it.

"Runaway buggy!" someone shrieked from the sidewalk.

A chorus of shouts rose in the street. Among them was Side-Whiskers's angry cry. "Runaway slave! Somebody catch that black boy!"

Austin scrambled up to see Henry-James tearing up the road after the carriage.

"What on earth?" Uncle Drayton shouted. "That's my slave! Get him!"

"No!" Austin shrieked at him. "He's going after Charlotte! She's in the carriage!"

Uncle Drayton gave Austin one stricken look before he turned and bolted after them. Austin followed, feet tripping over the cobblestones as he tried to catch up.

Uncle Drayton's long legs gained on Henry-James as he

drove like a train car into an intersection strung with buggies and wagons. A large black coupe pulled away from the side of the road, just as the Dearborn careened toward it. Henry-James pumped past it and flung himself upward toward the horse, disappearing in front of the carriage. Austin stopped in the street, heaving for air, as the carriage, too, rocked to a halt.

Uncle Drayton caught up with it, ripped open the door, and pulled out a curled-up bundle with deer-colored hair. Several people on the sidewalk cheered. Eyebrows and Side-Whiskers bustled off toward their carriage, shaking their fists.

By the time Uncle Drayton reached the front of the Mills House again with a shaken Charlotte on one hip and Henry-James trailing along behind him, Austin saw that his face was set like stone.

He doesn't understand what's happened at all, Austin thought. *I'd better start talking—fast!*

"What I said in front of those men was a lie," he said as soon as Uncle Drayton was even within earshot. "Aunt Olivia sent us—there was a message from my father—she told us to bring it at once—but then those men stopped us at the dock—who are they anyway?—and they started to search Henry-James, but he had the message in his mouth, and he swallowed it so they wouldn't find it—and I know I promised not to lie any more, but I think this was an exception, don't you?"

Uncle Drayton blinked and shifted his eyebrows before he turned to Charlotte. "None of that explains what you are doing here, young lady. I'm sure your mother didn't send you." He cleared his throat. Austin was sure he heard him mutter, "It was outrageous enough that she sent these two."

Charlotte opened her mouth, but she couldn't seem to say anything.

Austin stepped forward. "Sir," he started to say.

But Uncle Drayton shook his head. "We shall deal with that later. I must find a way to get another message to Wesley to let him know his first one was destroyed." He frowned darkly. "Though I have no idea how I'm going to do that now that every secessionist zealot in the city is watching me."

"We'll think of something!" Austin said brightly.

"*You* will not do anything but sit in my hotel room until I find someone to escort the three of you back to Canaan Grove."

"But, sir—"

"Marse Drayton?" Henry-James stepped up next to Austin. The other three stared at him.

"May I can speak, sir?" he said.

"What is it?" Uncle Drayton said sharply. He fumbled for his pocket watch and flipped open its cover.

"I know what that there message said."

Uncle Drayton's head snapped up. Austin jolted a look at Charlotte. She stared back in terror.

"What do you mean, boy?" Uncle Drayton said.

"That message, from Massa Austin's daddy. He say don't let the South break off from the North, 'cause the North sure 'nuff gonna elect Marse Lincoln, and he ain't gonna stand for no see-seedin' no how."

Henry-James shifted his eyes to the ground. Swiftly, Uncle Drayton jerked the black boy's chin up with his hand.

"Did your missus tell you what that message said?" Uncle Drayton demanded.

Lie, Henry-James! Austin wanted to shout to him. *Just this once!*

But Henry-James slowly shook his head. Uncle Drayton's

voice lowered to a menacing growl.

"You read it, didn't you, boy?" he said. *"Didn't* you?"

With painful slowness, Henry-James nodded. And Austin and Charlotte watched in horror as Uncle Drayton drew his hand up over his shoulder and swung it like an ax across Henry-James's face.

Chapter Eleven

*I*f anyone stopped on the street to watch Drayton Ravenal slap his slave, Austin didn't notice. All he saw was the shame smeared like mud across Henry-James's face. And all he heard was a scream.

"Daddy, no! Don't hurt him!"

"You should have thought about me hurting him before you taught him to read." Uncle Drayton's voice was low and tight. Austin couldn't have been more frightened if his uncle had been yelling until his veins stood out. Every word cut into him like a hatchet.

But I have to say something! his own thoughts shouted at him. *I have to make this right!*

"You did teach him to read," Uncle Drayton said to Charlotte. "Against my direct order, you went right on and did as you pleased—"

"It was my idea, sir," Austin said. "Don't punish her. Punish me—"

"*When* will you people stop telling me what I should do

and what I should think?" Uncle Drayton reached out and snatched Henry-James to him by his now-tattered shirt. "It is not a matter of punishment. It is a matter of refusing to have a slave I cannot trust."

Austin shook his head. "But, Uncle Drayton, I practically forced him—"

"Fine, then I will remove the temptation—"

"Please, Daddy!" Charlotte cried. "Don't say I can't see Henry-James."

"It does me no good to forbid you to do anything, Charlotte Anne," Uncle Drayton said through his teeth. "You do it anyway. No, this has gone far enough. I am taking him straight to Chalmers Street."

Charlotte's scream punctured Austin through the stomach. She threw herself at her father and clawed at his waistcoat.

"You can't, Daddy!" she cried over and over. "Please, no, please!"

Uncle Drayton peeled her away with both hands. "This will get you nowhere, Charlotte. Now stop it!"

"I don't understand!" Austin shouted over Charlotte's cries. "What is Chalmers Street?"

Uncle Drayton pulled Charlotte's face into his chest where she sobbed against his waistcoat. "That is where Ryan's Slave Mart is," he said. His voice sounded dead. "We are taking this boy there, and I do not want to hear a word about it from you."

He strode off like a stranger, pushing Henry-James ahead of him by the back of the neck. Charlotte clung to the tail of his frock coat and wailed as if her heart would break.

Austin stood rooted to the sidewalk. *Ryan's Slave Mart?*

his mind groped. *He's taking Henry-James to a slave mart? Why—?*

But of course there could only be one reason—and only one reason why Charlotte would howl like Bogie.

Henry-James was about to be sold.

Another scream pierced the air, and this time it came from Austin. "Uncle Drayton, don't! It's my fault! It's all my fault!"

But Uncle Drayton only turned from the corner and glared furiously. "You may come along, Austin," he said. "But only if you hush that mouth of yours. I believe you've said enough."

For once, Austin was sure he had.

The cobblestones of Chalmers Street clattered with passing wheels and horses' hooves, and the high, white buildings lining its sidewalks echoed the calls of busy Charlestonians.

Some people seemed to be hurrying on to other places with white oak baskets over their arms or newspapers tucked at their sides. But a throng of men were gathered in front of one building, each man stretching his neck and remarking to his neighbor.

Austin's mind was spilling over with his own confused and panicked thoughts as he pushed through the crowd behind Uncle Drayton. He heard only snatches of their conversations.

"They're clean enough—"

"They always are. Don't you know the speculators do that for show—"

"Make them dance—let's see how lively they are—"

"Don't want no lifeless darky—"

"Nor a lame one either. Look how that one limps—"

"The teeth tell it all. Let us see the teeth!"

As they broke through the clump of people, Austin saw at once what they were talking about, and his own thoughts choked off.

A line of black men, chained together by their arms, was trotting up and down in front of the building like a flock of frightened turkeys. Each wore nothing more than a thick cloth wrapped around him like a diaper, and their skin showed the gooseflesh produced by the chill of the late spring afternoon.

But it was the looks on their faces that grabbed at Austin's throat. Their eyes bulged and their lips trembled. They looked so ashamed.

He had never seen Henry-James look that way—ever.

Suddenly, the top half of the wooden front door was flung open and a red-faced bald man appeared, shaking both his head and his finger.

"What do you mean, paradin' them slaves in the street—that's against the law here!"

The man who held the chain barked back at him, "Since when?"

"Since four years ago when they passed a city ordinance! There's a yard in back and a barracoon where you can stall your property until it's time for them to go on the block—but get them out of the street before you get us all arrested."

The bald man slammed the door behind him. Austin felt the anger pounding in his head.

You can get arrested for parading them in the street—but not for slapping them or selling them?

In front of him, Uncle Drayton was headed for the door. Austin hurled himself forward and got in front of him as his uncle jerked on the handle.

"You can't do this, Uncle Drayton," he said.

"Step aside, Austin," he said, his voice still toneless.

"Henry-James is our friend—"

Uncle Drayton wrenched the door open, top and bottom, and pushed Henry-James inside. Charlotte still hung on to her father's coat as he stepped in.

"Well, you got your friend into trouble, didn't you?" he said.

"I'm—"

But Austin stopped, the words "I'm sorry" frozen on his lips as he followed Uncle Drayton into the dank, smelly room. *I can't say I'm sorry,* he cried out inside. *I'm not sorry! He's the one who should be sorry!*

"Now, gentlemen and fellow citizens," a voice boomed from the other end of the room, "here is a big, black buck Negro. He's stout as a mule."

Austin looked up and gasped. The red-faced, bald man stood to the side of a three-foot-high block of wood, waving his arms and smiling broadly at the crowd of men who littered the room. On top of the block was a handsome, broad-shouldered black man, wearing only a diaper and an expressionless face. He stared straight ahead as the bald man described him like a farm horse.

"Good for any kind of work," he shouted. "And he never gives any trouble. How much am I offered for him?"

"Four hundred," a man said calmly from his chair.

"Who will make it five?"

"Five hundred," said another man over the top of his newspaper.

"Do I hear six hundred? Come now, gentlemen, this is fine stock."

"Six-fifty."

Austin stared from one to the other, his head pounding. All it could hammer out was one thought: *They're buying human beings. They're buying human beings.*

On the other side of Uncle Drayton, Charlotte was crying into her hands. Henry-James stood in front of him, still as a cornered rabbit, and watched the "buck" go for fifteen hundred dollars. Austin felt vomit rising in his throat.

"Next!" the bald man shouted. "Here's a young black wench. How much am I offered for her?"

Someone shoved a girl the color of coffee with milk up onto the block. She was Kady's age, and she shivered and held out her hands to a wrinkled black lady still down on the floor.

"Stand up straight!" the bald man commanded her. "Let them get a look at you!"

The girl barely moved.

"What am I offered for her?"

"She's too yellow to take the climate!" one man called out. "One hundred and fifty."

"I hear one-fifty."

"She can still have babies, I don't care what shade she is," muttered a man behind Austin. "One seventy-five!" he called out loud.

"I have one seventy-five. Do I hear one-eighty?"

The men ignored him and set to chatting amongst themselves.

The bald man looked apologetically at the slave girl's owner and said dully, "Sold for one hundred seventy-five dollars."

A moan the likes of which Austin had never heard arose from the floor. The wrinkled black woman collapsed to the boards, shoulders trembling out of control.

"My baby!" she cried out. "Don't take my baby!"

"Mau-Mau!" the girl cried.

She thrust out her arms, but her new owner grabbed them and tied them behind her back. Without a word, he hauled her out the front door. The wrinkled black woman put her head back to the floor and sobbed.

Austin felt as if his stomach were being ripped in two. He put his hand up to his mouth to keep from throwing up.

"That's all I have on the bill for today, gentlemen," the bald man said. "Are there any other sales?"

"Right here," Uncle Drayton called. His voice remained lifeless, but his back was straight and his chin set as he took Henry-James solidly by the arm and pulled him forward.

"Mr. Ravenal!" the man said. "We don't see you here much." He looked admiringly at Henry-James. "It looks like your presence was worth waiting for. This is a fine piece of merchandise! Would you step over here and give me some of the particulars before we open the bidding?"

Uncle Drayton let go of Henry-James and bent his head with the bald man's. Austin fought down his nausea and inched closer to Henry-James. He could hear Charlotte's wrenching, smothered sobs behind him.

"Limp," Austin hissed without moving his lips. "Pretend."

Henry-James didn't look at him. Austin could feel his hard, rigid shaking, and he saw a wildness in his eyes. Fear whipped up in his chest.

He's too scared to hear me. He's gone now—for sure.

"Next!" the bald man called out.

With the awful slowness of a bad dream, Henry-James was dragged up onto the box, and his chin was jerked up by the red-faced man's rough hands. The men in the room looked up with interest and droned out orders to the auctioneer.

"Open his mouth. Let's have a look at his teeth."

"Bend him backward. Does he have a strong back?"

"I'll start at two hundred—"

"No!" Charlotte screamed it so loud the bidding halted. All eyes watched as she frantically waved her hands as if she no longer knew where to put them without Henry-James there. "No, Daddy, please!" she screamed again.

Uncle Drayton's color drained, but he pulled Charlotte's face against him and nodded to the bald man. "Go on with the bidding," he said.

"Before I bid," said a white-haired gentleman, scraping back his chair, "I want to see the darky walk. I never buy a slave without seeing him walk."

The red-faced man glowered at Henry-James as if he should have thought of that himself. "Walk, boy," he said.

Austin closed his eyes to hold back the tears. *That was our last hope,* he thought miserably. *And he was too scared to hear me.*

A low growl ran through the room, and Austin opened his eyes.

"He can barely move!" the white-haired gentleman cried. "What are you trying to sell us, Ravenal?"

Austin felt his chin drop to his chest. In front of the block, Henry-James was tripping and stumbling, his left foot barely touching the floor before he brought it up and appeared to wince with pain.

"What is this?" Uncle Drayton said. "I've never seen the boy limp before!"

"It must have happened just today," Austin piped up. "He's been through a great deal, you know, not the least of which was that run up Meeting Street after the carriage—and stopping the horse and all—"

"Damaged goods, Ravenal," the bald man said. "I don't think you'll get a sale here. Am I right?"

There was a murmur of agreement, and the bald man gave Henry-James a shove. "Go back to your master, boy," he said.

Henry-James didn't look at any of them as he slipped over to join them. Charlotte bit her hand and darted her eyes from Henry-James to her father and back again.

Uncle Drayton snatched the slave boy up by the arm and half dragged him out the front door and into the street. Austin followed with Charlotte, trying hard not to smile.

But when they got to the corner, Uncle Drayton stopped. He shook Henry-James—hard—and Austin felt the grin drop from his mouth.

"You haven't heard the last of this, boy," Uncle Drayton snarled at him. "As soon as we get back to Canaan Grove, you will go into confinement." He tightened his grip, but his eyes went straight to Austin. "And he will stay there," he said, "until he heals."

✢ ✢ ✢

Chapter Twelve

"**I** am just as angry as I know how to be!"

Austin believed that. He had never seen his gentle mother double up her fists or stomp around a room or flash her eyes like she was doing now. The way she was marching back and forth in front of the fireplace would have pumped up his own anger—if he hadn't felt as flat as the soles of his own shoes. He watched her and tried to breathe around the lump that had become lodged in his throat on the boat ride back to Canaan Grove.

"Drayton is lucky he didn't come back with you all," she said stormily. "If I could get my hands on him, I would shake him until his teeth rattled! I was never even told my son was being sent to Charleston—in a storm—"

"Aunt Olivia said she told you," Austin said.

"She never did anything of the kind!"

"Now Miss Sally, you shouldn't be gettin' yourself all riled up like this. It ain't good for what ails you."

Austin looked at Ria, who was standing, arms folded, in

112

the corner. But he quickly dropped his eyes to his lap. He'd felt her angry gaze drilling into his back ever since he'd come in.

Of course she hates me, he thought miserably. *I hate me, too! It's my fault Henry-James is locked up who-knows-where. It's my fault he's going to be sold.*

He squirmed on the brocade chair and wiggled his knees back and forth. *But I was right. I was!*

He waited for the energy of anger to pummel in his mind. But his head felt too heavy—and too bruised by the looks Ria was pounding at him.

"Come on now, Miss Sally," Ria said. "You gots to lie down—"

"How can you be so calm, Ria!" Mother said. "This is your son we're talking about!"

Ria moved soundlessly to the bed and pulled back the coverlet. "Well, my son shouldn't oughta broke the law, should he?"

Her gaze skimmed roughly over Austin. *Nor yours either,* her eyes said. Austin swallowed hard against the lump in his throat.

"He has courage, Ria," Mother said, her face flushing. "You can't fault him for that."

"Courage ain't gonna do him no good now, is it?" Ria said woodenly. "He locked up somewhere, waitin' to be sold."

Mother swept over to the bed and grabbed Ria's arm. "That isn't going to happen. I'll see to it," she said. "As soon as my brother returns from Charleston—"

"No, Miss Sally." Ria pulled away and looked Mother straight in the eye. "You only gonna make it worse. Just let it be."

Mother shook her head until her night bonnet slipped sideways. "I never thought I would hear my Ria talk like that."

"How else I'm s'pose to talk?" Ria said. "You always think the best thing gonna happen, and Miss Sally, sometimes it just ain't. I wish you would just let it be."

Austin's mother looked at her for a long time. It felt to Austin as if they were having a conversation without saying a word.

"You need anything more tonight?" Ria said finally.

Mother shook her head.

"I'm gonna go on back to Daddy, then. He 'bout to die thinkin' 'bout the boy locked up."

That stabbed at Austin. He dug his eyes into the palms of his hands until Ria closed the door behind her.

"Austin," his mother said.

Austin looked up to see her sagging onto the bed as if someone had poked a hole in her and all her energy was escaping through it. He hurried over to her, and she wilted against him. He helped her get under the covers.

She closed her eyes, and Austin felt his hands begin to sweat. She'd never looked quite so pale and tired before.

"I want you to write a letter to your father for me," she said. "Aunt Olivia's girl, Mousie, will see that the stagecoach driver gets it when he comes by."

Austin sat uneasily on the side of the bed. "What do you want me to say?"

"Tell him to prepare to come for us."

Austin's neck jerked. "Come for us? You mean, take us back up north?"

She nodded fretfully. "If I cannot talk any sense into your uncle, then being here is worse than being with no family at all. I would rather lie in bed in a dingy hotel room in Baltimore than be surrounded by all this elegance knowing the brutality that is going on right under my window."

She breathed hard, as if saying that had taken everything out of her. Austin breathed hard, too—in panic.

"But I don't want to leave here!" he said. "It's my fault this happened."

"It's Uncle Drayton's fault—" she began. But her eyes drifted closed, and she traced a finger over the top of his hand. "Write and tell Father," she whispered. "It's the best thing."

And then her transparent eyelids flickered, and Austin knew she had fallen asleep. His own mind was wide awake—and pounding once again.

I hate Uncle Drayton for this. I'll never forgive him! it shouted at him. *But I have to make it right. I can't leave. I can't write to Father—until I make it right.*

Or I'll never forgive myself either.

It was one thing to make a decision that felt strong and sure in his head, and another to know how to carry it out. Austin tossed and turned over it all night, and he was awakened from a fitful sleep at dawn by the bellowing of a faraway horn.

That's Daddy Elias, waking up all the slaves, he thought sleepily.

It was a welcome sound—like it was telling people just what they needed to do. Austin sat up and swung his feet over the side of the bed. If anyone could tell him, it was Daddy Elias.

The sluice gates in the rice fields had been opened and

the flow of water allowed to flood them. While they waited for
the seeds to sprout, the slaves had been shifted to higher
ground to plant the crops the Ravenal family would eat for
the next year—the white and sweet potatoes, the corn and
the collards and the peas. *I want to be eating them come
summer,* Austin thought as he hurried there, barefoot with
his pantaloon suspenders pulled up over the shoulders of his
underwear suit. *If I can fix all this, I will be. I won't have to
write to Father.*

He found Daddy Elias standing in one of many circles of
slaves who were dipping pieces of corn cake into cans and
pulling out mouthfuls of hog and hominy. They swatted
listlessly at the early bees that hovered to inspect their break-
fasts, and there was no laughter and singing today. The sad
stillness filled up the lump in Austin's throat.

*What if Daddy Elias doesn't want to talk to me? What if
he's just as mad at me as Ria is?*

But when the old man saw him, his face softened into its
spoon-shaped smile.

"Good mornin', Massa Austin!" he said. "You up with the
early birds!"

"I came to tell you I'm sorry!" Austin blurted out. "And I
want to know what to do to make it better!"

The ring of slaves closest to Daddy Elias moved off a few
steps, casting doubtful, wide-eyed glances at Austin. Daddy
Elias softly nodded his frosty head and teetered, stiff-legged,
away from them. Austin followed, gulping at the lump.

"What you got to be sorry for, Massa Austin?" Daddy
Elias murmured to him, his crinkled face near Austin's ear.
"Jesus put some guilt in your soul?"

"Jesus?" Austin said. He could feel his eyebrows knitting.

"Jesus be your friend, don't He?" Daddy Elias said. "Didn't you take His friendship long 'bout a few months ago?"

Austin felt stunned. He slowly shook his head. "I did," he said. "But I haven't been a very good one. I don't think He wants to talk to me anymore."

"What you talkin' 'bout, Massa Austin?"

Austin looked at him quickly. It was the first time he had ever heard anything sharp in the old man's tone.

"I've made a mess of everything, that's what I'm talking about," Austin said. "I talked Henry-James into learning to read. He didn't want to at first. I let Charlotte find out, and now she's in trouble. I let Uncle Drayton find out, and now Henry-James is locked up and we don't even know where he is."

"And Jesus say you got to take all that on your head?" Daddy Elias said.

"I don't *know* what Jesus says!" Austin said impatiently. "I haven't talked to Him since—" He let his mind flip back quickly. "For a long time."

"Mmmm-mmmm," Daddy Elias said.

Austin felt the anger pounding in his head again. "I need to know what to do now to make this all right again, Daddy Elias!" he cried. "I thought you could tell me."

"I am tellin' you," the old man said. "You can't make nothin' right till you puts it all on Jesus."

"I don't know how," Austin said. He felt stubborn, and he crossed his arms over his chest with a huffing of his breath.

"That's 'cause you got so much hatin' goin' on in you," Daddy Elias said. "Can't nobody hear Jesus when they's so busy holdin' hates in they hearts."

"Elias!" a voice trumpeted from across the field. "Why are these slaves standing around idle?"

Daddy Elias snapped his head around and at once started toward the figure on horseback who was silhouetted against the low sun. Austin felt his jaw muscles tightening.

It was Uncle Drayton, back from Charleston and already yelling at everyone.

I do hate him, Austin's thoughts drummed at him. *He makes everything wrong.*

And I'm going to make it right.

But his shoulders slumped as he headed away from the vegetable field. Where could he even start if Daddy Elias wouldn't tell him? Who would even listen to him now that he'd tangled everything up so badly?

Suddenly, he felt something wet and cold against his hand. He jerked it away and looked down to see a brown face with too much skin looking back at him. Bogie's eyes drooped as he dropped his haunches to the ground. A pleading paw came up and patted Austin's knee.

"Bogie!" Austin said. He squatted down and took the dog's big head in his hands. Bogie leaned against him and sighed.

"You miss Henry-James, don't you?" Austin said. "I'm sorry, boy. Are you gonna forgive me?"

Bogie grumbled low in his baggy throat and pawed forlornly at Austin's chest. Austin tugged at his jowls. "I would take you to him—I would—but I don't even know where he is."

A light glinted in Bogie's eye, and he stood up. His stick of a tail switched intently back and forth.

"I told you, I can't take you to him. I don't know where he is," Austin said. The lump was getting so big that he could barely talk. He was afraid he was going to cry.

Bogie, on the other hand, threw his head back and howled at the sky. Then he romped a few steps away and came back and put his mouth around Austin's wrist.

"Don't bite me!" Austin said.

But Bogie let go, ran a little farther, and came back and pawed him. His tail wagged—like it had a purpose.

"You know where you want to go, don't you, Bogie?" Austin said. "Do you know where Henry-James is?"

As if in answer, Bogie spun himself in three circles and bounded toward the shops. Heart racing, Austin took off after him.

The carpentry and coopering and tanning shops were all alive with activity as they drew near. Bogie stopped, sniffed the air, and then slunk down to the ground like a snake. Austin flopped to his stomach and followed him, pulling himself behind the shops by his elbows. At the end of the row, where a small, shabby building with only one high window stood slightly apart from the others, Bogie stopped—and he began to whine.

"Is that where he is?" Austin whispered.

Bogie whimpered again and inched himself closer to the shed. Hardly daring to move at all, Austin slithered behind him until he was up against the bedraggled shack. He pressed his mouth against a crack and hissed, "Henry-James."

From inside there was a thud. In a voice he could barely hear, someone said, "Massa Austin?"

Bogie gave a joyous yelp. Austin clamped both hands over his muzzle and looked wildly around. The shop sounds went on uninterrupted.

"Yes," Austin hissed through the crack. "And Bogie."

To prove it, Bogie scratched happily at the side of the shed.

"I'm so sorry, Henry-James—" Austin whispered into the crack.

But Henry-James cut him off with a sharp, *"Shhh!"*

Austin stiffened and listened. From beyond the shed, near the tanner's, he heard a trumpeting voice.

"This bridle fell apart in my hands while I was riding back from Charleston!" a man was bugling. "I could have been *killed* by your carelessness!"

"Uncle Drayton!" Austin whispered to Bogie.

"Get away 'fore you gets caught!" Henry-James muttered into the crack.

"I'll be back when it's safe," Austin hissed.

And he ignored the black boy's "no!" as he crawled off behind Bogie.

Once out of Uncle Drayton's earshot, Austin tore like a low-flying duck toward the rice fields with Bogie bounding at his side.

"We have to find Charlotte and tell her!" Austin called to him as they careened around the garden hedges to the spot where they had lessons.

But neither Charlotte nor Kady was there. And calling—and howling—to them produced nothing.

"Come on!" Austin said to Bogie, and they flew off toward the Big House. Bogie bounded up the back steps with Austin and dropped himself expectantly at the door.

"Wait here," Austin told him. "Aunt Olivia would have you cooked for lunch if she found you in the house."

Austin slid into the back hall and poked in and out of the

rooms, all empty of people except for the slaves polishing the floors on their hands and knees—until he skidded to a stop at the bottom of the front stairs.

Polly was sitting there—with Tot clinging to her, of course. When Polly saw Austin, she sprang up and locked her claw hands around his arm. He was too surprised to pull away.

"Boston—" She gave her head a frenzied shake. "Austin, I've been waiting for you."

"Why?" Austin said bitterly. His head commenced to pounding, and he wrenched his arm away. "So you can gloat?"

"I don't even know what that means," she said, her voice nervous and shrill. "I just wanted to tell you something— something Tot knows."

Austin flitted his eyes over the cowering black girl. "Unless she knows where Charlotte is, I don't care about anything she knows—or you."

"You'll care about this," Polly said. "Tot knows where they're keeping Henry-James. She takes his supper to him. She's the only one who's allowed to see him."

In spite of himself, Austin's eyes widened. "Why Tot?"

Polly looked painfully down at the floor. "Because Mama thinks I hate all of you—Charlotte and you and Henry-James. She thought she could trust my slave girl."

Austin stiffened. "Can she?"

Polly shook her head. "But you can," she said.

"Why should I?" Austin said. "You're the one who got Kady in trouble. You tried to do it to Charlotte, too. Uncle Drayton never would have suspected Henry-James could read if you hadn't blabbed about the alphabet blocks."

"Then just never you mind, Boston Austin!" Polly burst

out. Her ruddy face burned redder than ever. "For once I was trying to make up for something, and you're too high and mighty to accept my help!"

She thrust her tongue out at him and snatched up her skirts. Tot dove to lift them for her and brought the back one all the way to her waist. Polly squealed and slapped it down, and then she flopped to the bottom step, put her face in her hands, and cried. Austin felt his shoulders sag.

"Don't . . . don't do that," he said miserably.

She wailed on. Austin squirmed in his shoes.

"All right," he said. "You can help by . . . by just not telling Aunt Olivia that I know."

Polly nodded and kept sobbing. Austin fled to look for Charlotte.

He found her in the music room, her eyes red and swollen.

Is there anyone who isn't crying today? he thought. But he leapt across the room to her and squatted at her feet.

"Lottie!" he whispered to her. "I know where he is!"

Charlotte's puffy eyes swelled, and she searched Austin's face. "Henry-James?" she said.

"That's right!" Austin said. His head pounded out a rhythm he could almost dance to. "And tonight, I'll take you to see him!"

"Oh no, you won't, Austin Hutchinson," said a voice above him.

He looked up to see Kady standing there. Her brown eyes were smoldering as she took him by the shoulder. "Oh no, you won't go see him."

✢ ⋅✢⋅ ✢

ustin stared at his cousin. It was the first time he had seen any life in her eyes for weeks—and now she sounded as bitter as everyone else.

"I thought you were on our side!" he said.

"I am," Kady said. "You didn't let me finish."

Austin's mind knotted in confusion. Beside him, Charlotte was shaking her head.

"I have to go see Henry-James, Kady!" she said.

"I know, so let me finish." Kady beckoned them with her hands, and they both crowded close to her. "Don't you dare go see Henry-James—wherever he is—unless you set him free."

"Let him go?" Austin cried.

"Shhh!" Kady hissed at him. "You are a bright boy, but you have a mouth bigger than South Carolina."

"You want us to free him?" Charlotte whispered.

"I'd do it myself if they weren't watching me like a bunch of overseers," Kady said, pulling her hands into angry fists. "I would do anything to get back at Daddy for what he's done!"

As he watched Kady's eyes glitter, Austin heard something rustle through his mind. *"You got so much hatin' goin' on in you."*

He shook the thought out of his head. A slow pounding was taking its place. *Listen,* it said. *Someone is finally telling you what to do. Someone you trust.*

"All right," Austin said to her. "That's what we'll do. We have to wait until it's dark, but then we'll sneak out there, open the door, and he'll be free. That will solve everything. He won't be sold, he can read and write all he wants, he can go away and—"

"We'll never see him again," Charlotte said. Her eyes swam.

"Let's not worry about that just yet," Kady said to her. "Turn him loose, and we'll think of something. You just let Henry-James go—and tell him not to wander too far away."

Charlotte's face brightened at that. "All right," she said. "As long as it's that way. We'll take him blankets and some clothes—"

"I have some that will fit," Austin said. And then his heart sank again. "But how do we keep the Patty Rollers from finding him if he's going to hide nearby?"

"They know his face now," Charlotte said. "Don't you remember last winter? Irvin Ullmann said he would always be watching for him, and if he found him he'd—"

She stopped and shuddered. But a mischievous gleam came into Kady's eyes.

"They wouldn't bother if they got a glimpse of a white boy, would they?" she said.

"No, but what does that matter?" Austin said. "Henry-James is black."

Kady wiggled her eyebrows. "Not if we steal some of Polly's magic beauty secrets."

Austin felt his face brighten. "We don't even have to steal them," he said. "I think I can get Polly to give me some—as much as I want."

Charlotte and Kady both stared at him.

"Why?" Kady said.

"Well, see—"

"Wait," Charlotte said. She gave a disappointed sigh. "That won't work. What's going to happen when they find out Henry-James isn't where he's supposed to be anymore? They'll search everywhere."

"Then we have to find a way to keep them from finding out, that's all," Kady said. She rolled her eyes. "Right—that's all. How on earth—?"

But once again Austin smiled. "I think I know how to solve that one, too," he said. "May I go now, Kady? I have to find Polly—and Tot."

With Bogie sniffing ahead of him, Austin found the two of them in the kitchen building, washing Polly's face in buttermilk. She yanked her face out of the bowl and began to snarl as soon as she heard Austin's voice, but he got right to the point. As soon as she discovered she now had the upper hand—and as soon as she got the milk off her face—she took a few minutes to toy with Austin's patience. But he outlasted her, and finally she and Tot agreed to his plan.

He left the kitchen building an hour later with three bags of crushed egg shells and a promise from Tot.

"You're going to have a little more to eat for a while," he told Bogie happily as he headed back to the Big House. "But for now, you just have to wait for night to come."

But it seemed like it never would. Once he had gathered some clothes for Henry-James, and as an afterthought, some books for him to read, the afternoon dragged on like it was pulling a weight behind it. Finally, supper was over with, and Austin went to his mother's room as always to read the Bible with her. He found her already sleeping restlessly. Shrugging, he pulled one of the wing-backed chairs up to the window and watched the sun sink by unseen inches behind the trees.

I'm glad she's not awake, Austin thought, forehead pressed to the glass. *She'd spot what we're going to do right away.*

And she'd also ask me whether I've written that letter to Father.

Austin squirmed a little at that thought. After all the promises he'd made about lying and sneaking—after how clear it had all seemed just a few months ago that if you did what was right there was no reason to lie or sneak around—

After how good a friend Jesus has become—

Austin twitched. Where had that thought come from? He'd already told Daddy Elias he hadn't been a good friend to Jesus, that he hadn't talked to Him in a long time.

"That's 'cause you got all that hatin' goin' on," the old man had said.

Slowly, Austin's head began to rumble again. *I do!* he thought angrily. *I can't help it! Uncle Drayton has made it* impossible *to do what's right—without first doing what's wrong!*

"Somehow, Jesus," he whispered into the windowpane, "I don't think You'd agree with that."

It made him sad—and that didn't feel as strong as anger.

He got up with a start and peered out into the evening.

It's dark enough, he decided. *Time to go get Charlotte and Bogie.*

There wasn't a soul stirring near the shops as the three of them slunk through the shadows toward the shed.

"It's where they used to keep the tools," Polly had explained to him that afternoon. *"It's all shabby and nasty now."*

All the more reason to get Henry-James out of there, Austin thought.

Bogie lowered his nose to the ground and, tail smacking purposefully back and forth, padded straight to the back of the toolshed.

"Here?" Charlotte whispered.

Austin nodded.

"This is horrible!"

"But we're going to get him out," Austin whispered.

From inside the shed, there was a soft thump. Charlotte and Austin plastered themselves against the side of the building, and Bogie got up on his hind legs and scratched at it with his paws.

"Henry-James," Austin whispered. "It's us."

"I tol' you not to come out here," Henry-James whispered back. "You only gonna make things worse."

"No," Charlotte whispered excitedly into a crack. "We're going to let you out!"

"Miss Lottie?"

"Yes!" she said. "Go to the door."

"Ain't gonna do you no good," Henry-James whispered.

But Austin grabbed Charlotte by the arm and slid with

her around the corner to the front of the shed. Bogie led the way, tail wagging importantly.

When the door came in sight through the darkness, however, Austin stopped, and his heart took a dive.

"What's wrong?" Charlotte said. She peeked around him—and she saw it, too.

"That's the biggest lock I ever saw!" Austin hissed.

"I tried to tell you," Henry-James hissed from inside. "How else you think Marse Drayton gonna keep them other darkies from settin' me free?"

Austin frowned at the heavy brass padlock that held the door hasp in place. He grabbed it and yanked it, but it didn't budge. He let it fall back against the door in disgust.

And then he had a thought.

"How did Tot get your supper to you tonight?" he whispered.

"Through the window," Henry-James whispered back.

"Can you get out that way?"

"If'n I could, don't you think I woulda done it by now? I can't git up to it."

It hadn't occurred to Austin that Henry-James would run away on his own. The thought sent a chill through him.

"We're going to get you out," Austin whispered, his mouth close to the shed wall, "but you have to promise to hide someplace close."

"Why? So's I can git caught again?"

Actually, Austin had no idea why. He wasn't sure he knew anything anymore—even whether the angry pounding was showing him the right way. The lump in his throat grew bigger and the tears threatened behind his eyes, and he flattened himself against the wall.

"Please, just promise, Henry-James," he whispered miserably. "I just have to make this right, that's all."

There was a long pause. Austin bit his lip and tried to swallow.

"All right, Massa Austin," Henry-James whispered finally. "Let's have us a look at that there window."

Austin, Charlotte, and Bogie moved to the side of the shed where a high, narrow window had been cut out, up near the roof.

Charlotte nodded toward a wooden bucket turned upside down on the ground. "That must be what Tot stood on," she said.

Austin pulled it under the window and stood on it. Stretching, he got his fingers to the bottom edge of the window.

"I sees you," Henry-James said. "But I can't reach."

"He needs something to stand on, too," Charlotte said. "All I brought were blankets—"

"Books!" Austin whispered shrilly.

He dashed for the bundle and pulled out five volumes he'd packed with the clothes. Standing on his bucket, he said, "Watch out below, Henry-James!" and pitched them inside—along with a bundle of clothes and three bags of crushed egg shells.

"What this for?" Henry-James whispered.

"To turn you into a white boy," Austin said.

He was sure he heard the black boy's throaty chuckle. In a few minutes, chalky white fingers appeared at the window. Austin touched them with his and felt better.

"What now?" Charlotte whispered anxiously.

"If we could just get him up higher, and he had something

to climb down on over here, I'm sure he could crawl through the window," Austin said. "Two ladders would be perfect."

Charlotte's brown eyes suddenly sparkled in the dark. "We've done this before, Boston!" she whispered. "Why didn't I think of it?"

Before Austin could get out the first question, she bent over and slipped her petticoat out from under her dress.

"Start ripping this into strips," she said. "I'll tie the two blankets together."

Austin felt his face slice into a grin. "We really are a good team, Lottie," he said.

Within minutes, they'd made two "ladders"—one from Charlotte's petticoat and one from the blankets she'd brought along. Austin got on top of the bucket once more and flung all but the end of the blanket rope inside the shed. He wedged the end of it firmly between two boards on the lower edge of the window.

"See if that will hold you," he hissed.

He saw the blanket pulled taut—but it didn't move.

"That's powerful strong," Henry-James whispered back.

Austin then took the petticoat rope from Charlotte and did the same thing with it, leaving it to trail down the outside of the shed. Bogie put his front paws up on the wall and sniffed at it. He whimpered up at Austin.

"It's all right, boy," Austin told him. "It'll hold him for a minute."

"You ready?" Henry-James whispered from close to the window.

"Ready!" Charlotte whispered back.

Even Bogie seemed to hold his breath as slowly the top of Henry-James's head appeared, and then his whitened face, and then his stocky shoulders clad in Austin's favorite blue-green shirt. He balanced himself on his chest in the window opening, and Austin saw his eyes shining in the night.

"All right," Austin whispered to him. "Grab on to this rope—and Charlotte and I will catch you if you fall."

"Get back, boy—you too, Miss Lottie," Henry-James hissed to them. "If anybody gonna get hurt, it gonna be me."

Obediently, both Austin and Charlotte backed away from the shed. Henry-James hiked himself out a little farther, filling the opening with his sturdy chest. He took hold of the petticoat rope with both hands and began to crawl, upside down, along the side of the building until only his feet were left inside the window. He was about to let go and swing himself down when Charlotte grabbed Austin's hand.

"I heard something!" she whispered. The last syllable disappeared in her throat.

Austin jerked his head and listened. Sure enough, there were footsteps approaching.

Austin bolted toward the building. "Someone's coming," he hissed to Henry-James. "Hurry!"

Henry-James kicked his feet out the window and flipped over, hitting the side of the building with a thud. The footsteps paused and then grew faster.

"Hurry!" Austin whispered. He gave the petticoat rope a yank. With a cruel ripping sound, it broke free, and Henry-James hurtled to the ground. The footsteps were by now just on the other side of the shed.

"They're going to find him!" Charlotte whispered almost soundlessly.

"You git 'em, Bogie!" Henry-James said through his teeth.

In a flash of brown fur and long teeth, Bogie flung

himself around the side of the building and sent up a ruckus of snarling and growling and barking like an entire pack of bloodhounds. When Austin looked back around for Henry-James, he was gone.

From the other side of the shed, Austin heard a piece of cloth tear, long and slow—and the footsteps retreated back down the path and away from the shops. Bogie reappeared around the corner, still muttering to himself. Austin collapsed against the shed wall.

"Good job, Bogie," he said. Bogie loped over to him and put his head against Austin's leg.

"What if whoever that was is going for help?" Charlotte said. Her face puckered anxiously. "We'd better get these ladders down and get home."

Austin nodded, still chuckling to himself. Finally—finally—he'd set some of it right.

Maybe Jesus and I are friends after all, he thought.

It was the first good feeling he'd had in a long time.

Chapter Fourteen

The good feeling lasted only until the next day at dinnertime. There were two anxious faces, trying not to *look* like anxious faces, at the table. Uncle Drayton didn't notice.

But then, he doesn't even look at any of us anymore, Austin thought. His head pounded just a little. *That's fine with me. No matter what, I'm never going to forgive him— ever.*

Aunt Olivia, however, was more observant.

"When is there going to be laughter at this table again?" she said, chins quivering with annoyance.

"I told you, Olivia," Uncle Drayton said, "our way of life is going to change."

He went sullenly back to his plate of ham and turnip greens and swatted his hand over it.

"The flies have started already," he said. "Where is Tot? She needs to get a peafowl feather and keep these bugs off our food."

"She's gone to take that slave boy his dinner," Aunt Olivia said.

Uncle Drayton's head came up with a jerk. "You've sent *her?* The girl is a bumbler!"

"I had my reasons," Aunt Olivia said. She smiled smugly at Polly, who smiled smugly back.

Austin felt suddenly uneasy.

The dining room door came open then, and a sweaty, heaving Tot thundered in, slamming the door so hard behind her that the teacups rattled.

Austin's eyes met Charlotte's. Even her freckles had gone pale.

"What on earth is it?" Aunt Olivia asked.

Uncle Drayton fixed his eyes on Tot. "Is there something wrong out there with that slave boy?"

Tot shook her head like a terrified chicken and tripped her way over to Polly. She whispered in her ear and then backed up against the wall, wide-eyed. Austin couldn't look at Charlotte. He set his fork down and didn't even try to breathe.

I've done it again, he thought in agony. *I tried so hard to fix it—and I've messed it up again.*

"Well?" Aunt Olivia said, looking imperiously at Polly. "What *is* it?"

"She says that mongrel dog of Henry-James's gave her what-for," Polly said. "She's afraid of dogs." She dipped her spoon in her pudding and smiled haughtily around the table. "Tot says the boy is safely imprisoned and fed, and all is well." She sniffed. "And you all doubted my slave girl. I guess she showed you."

"You never see the boy without that smelly animal," Aunt Olivia said. "We should have locked him up, too."

Austin thought he would dissolve into a puddle. As it was, he didn't dare look at Charlotte. But he felt a nudge at his elbow.

Polly was smiling into her pudding.

"I thought surely Tot or Polly was going to tell," Austin said to Charlotte that afternoon when they were lying on their stomachs in the grass by the rice mill pond. All the trees were in bloom now and the air smelled of cherry blossoms and honeysuckle—and Bogie's breath. He lay between them, still licking his chops from the chipped beef Tot had fed to him instead of to Henry-James.

"The way she came in, all out of breath and scared-looking, I just knew she was going to scream it out that Henry-James was gone from the shed." She sighed. "It's still all right now, isn't it, Boston?"

Austin came up on his elbows. Things were tugging at him, too. *What if Uncle Drayton decides to sell Henry-James tomorrow? What's going to happen then?* He couldn't say that to Charlotte.

Charlotte knitted her eyebrows together. "I wish things could be the way they were before."

"Before what?" Austin said.

Charlotte sat up and took her apron thoughtfully into her hands.

"You're going to start wrapping that around your finger, aren't you?" Austin said.

She shrugged.

"Every time you do that, it's because you're getting upset," Austin said. "You wish things were like they were before what?"

Charlotte pulled the apron firmly around her finger. "Before Henry-James learned to read," she said.

Austin sat up with a start. "Are you sorry we did it?"

"No—well, yes! I hate all this fussing and fighting. I hate . . . hating my own daddy. I think I hate everything but you and Henry-James and Kady—"

Bogie brought his head up and surveyed her solemnly.

"And Bogie," she said. She giggled softly and then sighed, flopping down on the grass. "I'm so mixed up, Boston."

Me, too, Austin almost said. But he bit that back. *I can't be confused anymore,* he thought. *I still have more things to make right. I made this whole mess, and I have to fix it.*

He looked over at Charlotte. A tiny tear had trickled out of the corner of one eye. Austin straightened his shoulders.

"Would it help if we found out where Henry-James is now?" he said.

Charlotte looked at him quickly. "Do you think we could?"

"I know we could."

"How?"

Austin pointed down at Bogie. "We have the best nose in the South—right here."

Charlotte began to smile again. "When?"

Austin wiggled his eyebrows. "Tonight. As soon as it gets dark."

A steady rhythm beat in Austin's head that evening after supper as he felt the plantation quieting down and the Big House settling in for the night.

We're going to see Henry-James, it seemed to say. *We're*

going to tell him that no one knows he's gone yet—that he's safe—

Until when?

That thought stopped the beat like a stick in a wheel. Austin scowled as he opened his mother's bedroom door. *It's going to be all right,* he told himself firmly. *I have to make it all right.*

The energy pumped back into his head.

"That's a mighty sour face, Austin," his mother said drowsily from her bed. "Do you have lemons on your mind?"

There was a short grunt from the corner. Austin looked, and locked eyes with Ria.

"Ria's joining us tonight," Sally said. She coughed, a gravelly sound from deep in her chest.

"Your mama ain't been doing well today," Ria said as she bustled to the pitcher for a tumbler of water. "I ain't leavin' her when she got the fever like she do."

Austin went anxiously to his mother. Her face looked as pale as the lace-edged pillowcase, and there were dark circles under her eyes. Austin felt a flicker go through his chest.

"Are you sicker?" he said.

"No, I think I'm just weary of this place. I'll be so glad to hear from your father—and know when he plans to come for us."

Austin pulled his eyes from her face and poked his finger into the feather bed.

"Thank you for writing to him for me, Austin," she said. "I don't even have the strength to dip a pen in an inkwell." Her voice faded, and her eyes fluttered closed. Austin felt his cheeks burning as he watched her. He hadn't written to his father for her. He'd never even intended to—not until things were fixed.

But she seemed to be counting on it.

"Mother?" he whispered.

There was no answer. Austin lunged forward and took her by the shoulders. "Mother!" he cried.

A hand gripped his arm and pulled him back. "She just sleepin', Massa Austin," Ria said quietly. "You go on and let her rest now. That's what she need."

Reluctantly, Austin backed away from the bed. He felt Ria watching him.

"You love your mama, don't you?" she said.

"Yes," Austin said. He stared at her. "She's my mother."

Ria's eyes grew hard. "How would you feel if'n she was to all of a sudden be taken away from you? You right smart. You knows more'n most grown folks I knows, but if'n' she wasn't here no more—"

"Is she going to die?" Austin cried.

The hard look disappeared from her eyes, and she shook her head. "No, Massa Austin, she ain't gonna die. But you all the time askin' questions. How 'bout if you answer mine—'scuse me for sayin'."

The lump suddenly reappeared in Austin's throat. "I'd feel awful. I'd feel like—"

He couldn't say it. He could only see it—that moment at Ryan's Slave Mart when the cream-colored slave girl had been sold away from her "mau-mau"—for one hundred and seventy-five dollars.

Austin swallowed hard. "You're not really talking about me, are you, Ria?"

Ria shook her head. "No, I ain't. Henry-James, he's about a man now—workin' in the fields, takin' care of his grandpappy and me. But in here—" she put her hand to her chest "—he ain't no more growed up than any the rest of us. Each other's all we got, Massa Austin. Ain't nothin' gonna take the place of that. Nothin'."

"I'm sorry, Austin," Mother murmured. "I missed the Bible story, didn't I?"

Austin hurried over to her. "It's all right," he said. "I'll read it tomorrow."

When he turned back around, Ria had her back to him, preparing Mother's medicine. Austin slipped out of the room.

Charlotte was waiting under the back stairs with her eyes sparkling from within the hood of her green cape. On the back porch, Bogie was impatiently switching his tail to and fro.

"We're ready!" Charlotte whispered. "This is a real adventure, Boston!"

But Austin's chest felt heavy as they slipped through the shadows to the toolshed. Nothing seemed clear and strong and sure now. There was no steady rhythm of angry energy in his head, no exhilarating feeling that he was right. There was a tangled knot of confusion.

I was right to teach Henry-James to read! But it got him into trouble.

I was right to set him free. But now he can't see his family—he may never see them again!

I have to fix it. But I can't—I can't!

"Do you think Bogie can really pick up the trail from here?" Charlotte whispered.

Austin looked at the toolshed. *I wish we could go back to the way things were, too!* he wanted to cry. *But that was just as bad. I can't! I can't!*

"What's the matter, Austin?" Charlotte said. Her eyes were worried. "Don't you want to go find Henry-James?"

Bogie whined and nudged Austin with his paw.

"See?" Charlotte said. "You're the only one we can count on."

There was no energy in Austin, but he straightened his narrow shoulders. "All right, Bogie," he whispered. "Find Henry-James. Sniff him out, boy."

The twitching wet nose went to the ground and led Bogie in a wide circle. Austin watched his tail, which wagged slowly and uncertainly.

"Maybe he can't get the scent," Charlotte whispered.

And then the tail sprang to attention. Bogie grumbled low in his throat, and the tail began to vibrate—with a purpose.

"Here we go," Austin whispered.

And they were off.

There was no moon that night, and Bogie was no more than a shadow in front of them as they followed him—around the back side of the sugar cane mill, alongside the hog crawl, and into the tall grass that bordered the south end of the rice mill pond.

Henry-James was careful not to go in places where he could leave footprints, Austin thought. He looked around him and shivered. Snakes and alligators didn't leave footprints either. The low country could be spooky at night.

They came to a stop below the bridge, and Bogie sniffed cautiously at the water's edge.

"Do you think he went in the water?" Austin whispered.

"He can't swim, remember?" Charlotte said.

"Good, because I can't either."

"We know that," Charlotte said. She pointed. "Look, Bogie's found something!"

Bogie was rustling around in the jack-in-the-pulpit leaves. He splashed up out of the water and leapt onto a large, flat stone. With another bound, he reached another one, and then another.

"It's a stone path across the pond!" Austin said.

Charlotte was already on the first one and preparing to jump to the second.

"Please, Lord, don't let me fall in," Austin whispered. As he maneuvered his way down to the water, he tried not to notice that this was the first time he'd prayed to Jesus in a very long time.

The stones were slippery and covered with moss, but Austin managed to get from one to the other without tumbling into the pond. When he reached the last one, Bogie had already taken off. Austin followed Charlotte up along the other side of the pond, through more tall grass and a hillside crammed with azalea bushes, their blossoms all scattered on the ground below them.

"I saw these flowers from across the pond when they were in bloom in April," Austin whispered ahead to Charlotte. "We're almost to the rice mill. He wouldn't hide there."

"He isn't going there," Charlotte whispered back.

Bogie had, in fact, taken a sharp turn into a wilderness of cedars and oaks. Austin tried not to crash too noisily through the underbrush as he charged after him with Charlotte just ahead. Branches slapped at his face and the soft, uneven ground almost tripped him up. He was relieved when Bogie led them into a clearing and they stopped short at the edge of another, smaller pond.

Bogie whimpered at the water's edge.

"Now what?" Charlotte asked. Her eyes started to water. "I don't see him here."

Austin's heart sank. *If I can't even find Henry-James for Lottie, I really have messed everything up.*

Bogie suddenly let out a yip and threw his head back.

"Shhh, Bogie!" Charlotte hissed. "Don't howl!"

But Bogie was only sniffling at the air, and he obviously liked what he smelled. With one more happy bark, he charged into the water and galloped, splashing, straight out across the pond.

"What's he doing?" Charlotte said.

Austin peered out across the water, black and varnished-looking in the night. Its shiny surface seemed to stop and then start again.

"There's a little island out there," Austin whispered to her. "That's where he's going."

"But how did Henry-James get there?"

Austin felt his face cracking into a smile as he watched the dog. "Same way Bogie did," he said. "He walked."

For although only his head showed over the top of the water, Austin could see that Bogie was not swimming but running to the island. This pond was probably only about waist-high.

From across the water, Bogie gave a happy howl, which was followed by a firm *"Shhh!"* Charlotte snatched up her skirt and plunged into the water, high-button shoes and all. She was halfway to the island before Henry-James appeared. He was dressed only in Austin's dark brown pantaloons, rolled up above his knees, and he scooped Charlotte up and carried her back to where Austin stood, calf-deep in water and nearly crying with relief.

"You gonna get your white selves in trouble yet—and me, too!" Henry-James snapped at them. But his black eyes were brimming with sparkling, happy tears. Austin threw his arms around them both and hung on.

It was a magical moment, all surrounded by cricket chirps, frog belches, and Bogie's contented panting. It made all the confusion and the frightening thoughts and even the brooding plantation seem far away. Certainly it was a moment that was hard to let go of. But as soon as they were assured that Henry-James had berries and fish to eat and a blanket shelter to sleep in amid the little island's trees, he gave them a nudge back in the direction of the rice mill.

"You git on home now 'fore they starts lookin' for you," he said, trying to sound stern.

"Well, at least they aren't looking for *you*," Austin said. "We made sure of that." The moment had made him feel as if maybe everything *would* be all right.

Bogie, it seemed, wasn't so sure. Charlotte and Austin waited for him to lead them back through the woods, but he gave them only one look before he set off into the pond after Henry-James.

"No, boy," Henry-James said to him. "You gots to go back. These here chilrun be lost 'fore they takes two steps without you."

But it was Henry-James who looked as if he'd be lost—if Bogie left him there alone. He looked suddenly small and young, standing in the water with his dark island home behind him.

Austin heard Ria's words in his head: *"He ain't no more*

growed up than any the rest of us. Each other's all we got."

"Maybe Bogie should stay here with you," Austin called softly across the water.

For a minute, Henry-James watched his dog splashing eagerly toward him, and his mouth worked as if he were doing hard thinking.

Finally, he shook his head. "No," he said. "Bogie, you go on with the chilrun. Massa Austin your boy now."

"He's right," Charlotte said. "If anybody notices Bogie is gone, they'll know Henry-James is gone, too."

Bogie made a U with his body and chugged slowly back to Charlotte and Austin. He shook halfheartedly at the edge of the pond and looked back at Henry-James. But the black boy had already disappeared into the darkness. Bogie hung his head and led them the shorter way back to the Big House.

When they got there, Charlotte started up the back steps, but Austin caught her arm.

"We're soaking wet," he said. "We ought to get dry before we go in—or they'll have more questions than even I could ever dream up."

Charlotte nodded and pointed to the kitchen building. There was a trail of smoke coming from the chimney, and a lamp flickered in the window. It looked cheerful to Austin, and that was how he wanted to feel right now.

But the instant the door opened, he knew cheerful was something he wasn't going to feel for a long time.

Tot was sitting by the fire, sobbing and heaving so hard that her big lower lip was quivering like a saucer of jelly. Polly sat with her arm flung round her shoulders, and her thin face was as white as grits.

She sprang up when she saw them.

"It wasn't Tot who told Daddy!" she cried. "Honest! He found out on his own!"

Austin could barely move his mouth. "Found out what?"

Polly wrung her claw-hands together. "He found out, Austin. He found out Henry-James is gone."

Chapter Fifteen

"**N**o!" Charlotte cried. "He can't know!"

But Polly nodded until her limp curls flopped like shoelaces. "He does. Tot and I were out here making . . . well, it was a little while ago and he came storming in here with a pile of books. He was screaming at Tot, saying, 'Why didn't you tell me that slave boy was gone?' Of course, I told him she didn't *know* he was gone," she put in quickly. "And then he stomped out."

Tot moaned pitifully. Bogie whined nervously at Austin's side.

"Hush up now, Tot," Polly said. "You're not in any trouble." She pursed her lips at Austin. "But I can't say the same for you. He kept saying those books he had could only belong to you."

"Books?" Austin said. "What do my books have to do—?"

And then he knew, and so did Charlotte. Beside him, she gave a lost-sounding bleat.

"The ones you threw in there," she said.

146

Austin's heart flew to his throat, throbbing like a sore thumb.

"He'll whip me for sure now!" she cried. "He'll make me tell where Henry-James is, and then—"

She didn't finish. Austin couldn't let her.

"He doesn't have to know you were even part of it, Lottie," he said. "You wait here, and I'll go tell him I did it all on my own."

"You don't have to tell him anything. He's gone to Charleston." Polly sank back down next to Tot, the violet plaid of her skirt billowing up around her. "We heard him shouting orders to Isaac to harness the horses to the carriage."

"He *drove?*" Austin said. "That will take him hours!"

"He's going to need time—to calm down," Polly said. "I've never heard Daddy so riled up. I think we're all lucky he's gone." Her eyes darted to Austin. "You aren't blaming Tot for this, are you? She did just what you said."

But Austin didn't answer her. He turned on his heel and bolted for the door with Bogie bounding behind him. His foot tripped on the back stoop as he fled—and his thoughts tripped all over themselves.

It's not Tot's fault—it's mine! And I'll never be able to fix it now!

The Big House was dark and silent as Austin flung open the back door. Bogie looked up at him pleadingly with his red-rimmed, drooping eyes, but Austin slammed the door and stumbled up the back stairs.

I ain't no more "growed up" than anybody, either! he cried out hopelessly inside his head. And he pushed open his mother's door with both hands.

Ria was nodding in a chair by the bed. She fluttered up like a startled hawk and put a warning finger to her lips. Mother was breathing loudly in her sleep, and Ria was looking at him with the same suspicious gaze she always dropped on him.

She doesn't know yet, he thought. And that, at least, was good. But as he backed out of the room and shut the door, the lump in his throat nearly choked him. Who was there to go to—now that he'd run out of answers?

"Don't cry, Austin," a voice whispered behind him.

Austin's face whipped up to meet Kady's, framed by her dark, tousled curls.

"I heard about Daddy," she said. Her big eyes smoldered like coals. "He has even you ready to give up."

But the lump in Austin's throat began to disappear. "I won't give up!" he whispered to her. "But you have to tell me what to do next. You said if we just had Henry-James hide and not run away, it would be all right."

Kady shook her head. "I thought it would. I thought once Daddy had some time to think about it. . . . He seemed to be considering some other ideas. He even wrote to your father." She tightened her mouth into a grim line. "It looks like I was wrong. I'm just so mad I could spit!"

"But you have to help me!" Austin said. He glanced fearfully at his mother's door and lowered his voice. "We have to do something, and I don't know what. It's too confusing, Kady!"

But Kady only kept shaking her dark curls. "I'm in so much trouble already, I don't dare do another thing. I'll be lucky if Mama and Daddy don't marry me off to the next man who knocks on that front door."

Austin stared at her in disbelief. "You're giving up?"

"I'm facing facts, Austin," she said. "You're about the only person who's even free to move around anymore. As soon as Charlotte comes back in the house, Mama's going to have her under lock and key, too." She doubled her fists in front of her nightgown. "If Aunt Sally hadn't told her she'd already sent for Uncle Wesley, Mama would have the three of you on the street. It took me two hours to calm Jefferson down after he heard that—"

But Austin wasn't listening anymore. The lump rose in his throat again, and his heart began pounding.

"I have to do something," he said miserably. "But nobody will help me."

Kady let her fists fall to her sides, and her brown eyes lost their angry flame. "I'm sorry, Austin," she said. "I know you feel really alone. We've all dumped this on you. . . ." Her voice trailed off. There was no reason to stand there any longer, but Austin couldn't move. There was nowhere to go.

Suddenly, Kady took hold of his shoulders. "I do have one idea," she said. "Why don't you go talk to Daddy Elias?"

Austin looked miserably at his soggy shoe tops. "He'll just tell me to talk to Jesus."

"Oh," Kady said. She gave his shoulders a squeeze. "That's an even better idea."

For the second time that night, Austin crept down the back stairs and tiptoed to the back door. As soon as it opened, Aunt Olivia's shrill voice piped from the drawing room, "Charlotte, is that you?"

"No," Austin said, "it's me."

"Oh," came the cold reply. And that was all.

A chilly mist was descending on the plantation as Austin

crossed it toward Slave Street, Bogie following resolutely on his heels. He was sure he'd never felt more alone in his life, even a few months ago when he'd arrived at Canaan Grove, friendless and so different from everyone here that he'd been sure he'd never fit in.

This, he decided, was another kind of aloneness altogether. It was the lonesome feeling of everyone depending on him— when he knew he didn't have a prayer of making things right for them.

Even the slave cabins looked unwelcoming as they emerged out of the mist. Their glassless eyes seemed to be saying, "It's your fault our Henry-James will soon be off to the slave mart. It's your fault, boy."

Austin stopped on the dirt path and turned around. What was the use? Even his old friend couldn't fix this.

"Did you change your mind, Massa Austin?"

Austin looked up. He could just see a bent-over form through the fog, rocking back and forth on the porch of Henry-James's cabin.

"It's mighty lonesome in this here cabin," the old man purred. "Ain't nobody can fix lonesome like Massa Austin. Why don't you come on up here with some of them questions you always gots burnin' in your head?"

Slowly, Austin opened the creaky little gate and got himself to the steps. He sank down onto the top one and dropped his forehead in his hands. His elbows dug miserably into his thighs. Bogie licked Daddy Elias's hands and then dropped himself beside Austin.

"My, my, that there's a weighty load," Daddy Elias said. "What's you carryin', Massa Austin?"

"Everything," Austin said. And then, even though he told

himself it would do no good, Austin broke open like an egg and spilled the pounding, throbbing, heavy things inside him out at Daddy Elias's feet.

All the old man said when he was through was "Mmmm-hmmm."

"I have to fix it," Austin said, "but I don't know how, and I know you're going to tell me to ask Jesus, but I can't because it's my own fault and—"

"I ain't gonna say nothin' of the kind," Daddy Elias said. His voice was as soft and thick as the fog that enveloped them. "I was gonna ask you when Jesus tol' you that you had to fix it."

"He didn't tell me," Austin said.

"Then if'n He didn't tell you, I reckon it jus' ain't true."

"But I made the mess!" Austin protested. "I have to fix it!"

"Onliest thing you can do now is ask Jesus to forgive young Massa Austin for whatever he think he done wrong. And then you gots to let it go and count on the Lord to do the rest."

"How's Jesus going to forgive me?" Austin said. He twitched his legs back and forth. Bogie rose anxiously and poked him with his nose. "I don't even forgive me."

"Oh, now the Lord Jesus, He different from us," Daddy Elias said. His spoon-shaped smile grew wide as a ladle. "He *love* to forgive, if'n we asks Him to."

"Even if we haven't talked to Him in a while?" Austin said.

"Jesus, He know you new at this, Massa Austin, just like you was new at gettin' 'round this here plantation when you first come. And now, Henry-James, he say you ain't falled on your face or nothin' for nigh on two weeks now."

The mention of Henry-James grabbed Austin in the

chest. "Do you think Henry-James will forgive me if he gets caught—and sold?"

"You gonna forgive Marse Drayton if'n that happen?" Daddy Elias said.

"No!"

"Mmmm-hmmm," Daddy Elias said. "How 'bout we starts with the Lord first? He gonna take care all that, I knows."

"How do you know?" Austin demanded.

Daddy Elias rocked and patted Bogie's anxious head. "Some things we don't got to see nor hear," he said. "Some things we just knows." He shook one of Bogie's ears playfully. "Just like Bogie know his nose gonna take him where he got to go."

Austin nodded sadly. "Like Jefferson and his imaginary friend."

"That there Max-i-million fella Henry-James tol' me 'bout?" Daddy Elias chuckled. "That's right, Massa Austin. Jesus, He your frien' even though you can't see Him—even though you doesn't even talk to Him 'cause you tryin' so hard to be the sun and the moon." He chuckled again. "I think you gon' learn 'bout keepin' the Lord next to you this time, Massa Austin. Now you jus' ask Him to take away that down-guilty pinch out your heart. You jus' ask Him."

"Pray?" Austin said.

Daddy Elias nodded.

"Just like I do in my head?"

"Jus' like you's talkin' to Him."

Austin closed his eyes. It had been such a long time. Maybe Daddy Elias was wrong. Maybe Jesus didn't have time for boys who didn't have time for Him.

But as he bowed his head and squeezed his eyes shut

tighter, he felt something warm in his lap and something else warm on his shoulder. Bogie was nestled as close as he could get, and Daddy Elias was patting his arm. The touch seemed to say, "Go on, you can do it."

Austin blinked his eyes open. This felt like another time . . . when he'd sat with his friends and prayed. "Our Father," he and Charlotte and Henry-James and Jefferson had said together. And it had felt just like Jesus was there.

He is now, his head told him. There was no pounding rhythm. No anger. No energy to push him up, looking for the next thing to do.

He closed his eyes and said, "Jesus?"

It was quiet.

"He right there 'long side of you," Daddy Elias said softly.

"Jesus, I know I haven't talked to You in a long time, but I'm sorry for everything, and I'm sorry for all the things I've done wrong—the lying and the sneaking, even though I thought it was right then. And if Henry-James gets sold away from his mother and Daddy Elias because of me, please forgive me, because I know Charlotte and Ria never will."

He lifted his eyes and discovered they were filmy with tears that hadn't spilled out yet.

"Do I say 'Amen'?" he said.

"After I says thank you, Lordy, thank you for the precious heart of this here young'un. I know that there guilt, it ain't gonna eat him away no more 'cause You done chomped it all up. Now he ain't so heavy. Now he can set a spell while You does the rest." He smiled down at Austin. "Amen," he said.

And then he teetered up from his rocking chair. "Jesus gonna show you the way," he said. "You go on and see if He don't."

"How will I know?" Austin said.

"You gonna know like Bogie know his smells and Jefferson know that imagination critter. There ain't gonna be no questions in your head."

The fog was so thick as Austin and Bogie headed back to the Big House that Austin couldn't see farther than his outstretched arm. Bogie, on the other hand, put his nose to the ground and plunged ahead. Austin grabbed on to his tail and followed. Bogie took him right to the back door.

"I'm going to go in and go to bed now, Bogie," Austin whispered to him. "You get under the back porch and sleep."

He slipped inside the house and started for the stairs. Outside, a pitiful howl went up. Austin hurried back to the door.

"Quiet, boy!" he whispered hoarsely. "You'll wake up Aunt Olivia—and then there will be trouble for *you,* too!"

Bogie whined fitfully and pawed at Austin's knee.

"I know you're lonely, but—"

Bogie came up on his back legs and put both paws on Austin's shoulders. With his soft, furry face next to Austin's cheek, he gave a low, soft moan. The lump in Austin's throat grew even bigger.

"I think I feel that way, too," Austin whispered to him. "Come on."

He inched open the back door and squinted into the darkness. The house was still quiet. With his fingers to his lips, he pulled Bogie inside and soundlessly shut the door. The dog's toenails clicked on the wooden floor as they crept toward the back stairs.

I'd better carry him, Austin thought. He put his arms around Bogie's middle, but he couldn't budge him.

"You must weight 80 pounds!" Austin whispered. "Just try to walk quiet, then."

As if he understood, Bogie slunk down low to the ground and moved with Austin toward the steps. They'd just reached the bottom one when Bogie's ears came forward. He sniffed the air and whined.

"Is somebody coming?" Austin whispered to him. And then he heard it, too. Footsteps tapping furiously toward the top.

"Who's down there?" Aunt Olivia's voice said crossly.

Austin clapped his hand over his mouth and backed off the steps.

"Is that you, Austin Hutchinson?" she said.

Austin could see her shadow against the wall, double chin and all. On the balls of his feet, he leaped across the hall with Bogie slinking behind him. He dashed through the first doorway he found and closed it silently behind them. The smell of Uncle Drayton's books filled his nostrils as he leaned against the door and listened.

There was no sound. Bogie, too, leaned toward the door, and then he relaxed and began to sniff around the library.

Then I know she's gone, Austin thought, heart racing. For once, it felt good to know something for sure.

Still, he wasn't going to risk trying to get upstairs just yet. Bogie was going over the room with a thorough nose, and Austin sank into Uncle Drayton's desk chair. He'd spent a lot of hours in this room last winter, reading Uncle Drayton's books and planning adventures with Henry-James and Charlotte. He sighed unhappily.

That's probably all over now—one way or the other. Even if some miracle happens and Henry-James isn't sold, we'll probably be going back up north soon.

Austin got a pang in his chest. He still hadn't written the letter to his father. He hadn't even thought about it, as if he knew better than his mother what to do.

I should have done it, he thought.

And then he stopped. "I know," he whispered to Bogie. "There isn't a question in my mind. She told me to, and I know I should."

Bogie seemed content with that decision. He wormed his way between Austin's legs and flopped down under the desk at his feet. Austin scanned the desk for a pen, a piece of paper, and an inkwell.

The desk was messy, which was unusual for tidy, particular Uncle Drayton. Austin didn't see any paper at first, and he pawed through the confusion of pamphlets and letters. A pile of leaflets slid off onto the floor, and Austin leaned over to pick them up. The one on top caught his eye as if it had screamed at him.

The Education of Slaves, it said in bold black letters. *By Jefferson Davis.*

It was hard to read more in the dimness of the room. Austin located a candle and lit it by the coals that had been left dying in the fireplace. By the flickering light, Austin began to read.

Some of it was fancy gentlemen's language. Austin skimmed over that. But one sentence snagged him like a fishhook.

"Bogie," Austin whispered, "listen to this."

Bogie stirred restlessly under the desk and grumbled.

"'The slave must be made fit for his freedom,'" Austin read, "'by education and discipline, and thus be made unfit for slavery.'"

Austin's eyes slid down the page. "Jefferson Davis says he's educating his slaves right there on his plantation."

Bogie, of course, didn't answer. Austin's mind was speaking too loud to hear him if he had.

"I follow the lead of only one man besides myself—and that is Jefferson Davis!" That's what Uncle Drayton said. And Jefferson Davis says—

Austin turned back to the pamphlet. He'd come to the bottom of the page, but he couldn't open it. There was a seal holding it closed.

Uncle Drayton hadn't even read it yet.

"What do I do with this now, Jesus?" Austin whispered.

His friend was there—he could feel that. But Austin still didn't know what to do.

"Rest," Daddy Elias had said, "and He'll take care of it." But I have to write my letter.

He laid his cheek on the desktop. *But I'll rest first. And then I'll write.*

He closed his eyes, and he felt the room grow cozy around him.

There was light before his eyelids when he heard a voice say, "What in the name of heaven? What are you doing here?"

He blinked his eyes open to the sunlight—and the face of Uncle Drayton was right before him.

✢ ⚜ ✢

Chapter Sixteen

ncle Drayton's face wasn't the only one Austin saw as he jerked up and wiped the drool from the side of his face. Two men in frock coats and brocade waistcoats stood on either side of the library doorway.

One had eyebrows that met in the middle. The other wore side whiskers that stuck out from his cheeks like bear fur. Austin gasped.

"Can we never be free of this child?" Side-Whiskers said gruffly.

Uncle Drayton glared at him, but his eyes were just as aggravated as they settled on Austin.

"What are you doing in here?" he said. Austin opened his mouth to answer, but Uncle Drayton held up his hand. "I have no time for one of your long-winded explanations. Go on up to your room."

Austin started to get up, but at his feet, Bogie, too, began to stir. Austin slid a hand hurriedly under the desk and steadied the dog by touching his head.

Uncle Drayton turned impatiently to the two men, apparently forgetting Austin for the moment.

"If you are expecting any hospitality from me," his uncle said, "you will be disappointed. I did not invite you here."

"No," said Eyebrows, "in fact, you tried to escape when we ordered you to stop."

"Since when am I to take orders from you, Mr. Rhett?" Uncle Drayton said. "Just because your cousin has fashioned himself as the leader of your hotheaded secessionist group, that does not mean I am under any obligation to you."

"You have an obligation to the South to follow the majority!" Side-Whiskers cried, his thick face glowing red.

"I have an obligation to follow my own heart, Mr. Chesnut, though since your brother was a senator, you don't know how to do anything but hang on to the coattails of others!"

"I beg your pardon!" the whiskered Mr. Chesnut cried. "I stand for the South's right to rule ourselves as we wish—and so should you!"

"Is that why you tied my nephew and one of my slaves up like so much corn?" Uncle Drayton said bitterly. His eyes flickered over Austin again. Austin held fast to Bogie and to his own breath.

"With good reason," Mr. Eyebrows Rhett said. "I still believe you expected to receive Yankee information. In fact, I wouldn't be at all surprised, Mr. Ravenal, if you were a Yankee sympathizer yourself." His eyebrows twisted together. "We heard that your slaves have actually been taught to read."

"Who would tell such a preposterous lie?" Uncle Drayton said.

Mr. Rhett's face was smug. "At least three of the people

passing you in front of the Mills House that day who heard you shouting it for everyone to hear."

Austin dug his fingers into Bogie's fur. He watched his uncle's golden-tan face go white.

"Need I remind you," Whiskers Chesnut said, "that educating slaves is against the law?"

"No," Uncle Drayton said stiffly. "I am well aware of that."

Mr. Rhett drew himself up importantly. "It is not the law that I am concerned about," he said. "It is the honor of the South that I intend to uphold. How can we hope to gain our independence if we are not united from within?"

"Every Southerner worthy of respect believes in the Slave Code and supports secession," Mr. Chesnut said. He wheezed as if he'd run all the way from Charleston. "If you cannot do the same as men like Governor Pickens and Jefferson Davis—"

"I have followed the lead of Jefferson Davis to the letter!" Uncle Drayton said, his voice trumpeting. But Austin heard the tremor in it. Drayton pulled his hand from the desktop, and Austin saw the sweaty imprint he left there.

Austin's own mouth went dry. Mr. Rhett stepped forward and stood menacingly near Uncle Drayton's face.

"Jefferson Davis does not educate his slaves, Mr. Ravenal," he said. "Unless you can mirror his image, you have no right to call yourself a Southron."

"But Jefferson Davis does educate his slaves!"

All three heads turned. Three pairs of eyes looked, disbelieving, at Austin.

"Austin, hush up," Uncle Drayton said tightly.

"But it's true," Austin said. Gingerly, he let go of Bogie and picked up the sealed pamphlet. "It says so right here."

Side-Whiskers Chesnut snatched it out of his hand and

scowled at it, while Mr. Rhett read over his shoulder with his caterpillar eyebrows tied into a knot.

"Austin, what on earth?" Uncle Drayton said to him. "Go to your room, please, and for the last time, leave this business alone!"

As Austin rose from the chair, Mr. Rhett seized the pamphlet from his partner's hand and flung it down on the desk.

"Then Jefferson Davis, too, has lost his mind!" he cried. "Don't think you have heard the last of this, Ravenal."

Austin heard the last of it as he slipped past them and out the library door. His mouth felt full of cobwebs and his mind was still groping its way out of the tangle of sleep. He was up the back stairs and in his room before he realized Bogie was on his heels, sniffing warily at the air.

Quickly, Austin shut the door. He was suddenly wide awake.

"We have to find you a place to hide, boy," Austin whispered to him.

He ran his hand through his disheveled hair. Things were fast untangling themselves. Uncle Drayton was back. He knew Austin had set Henry-James free. The fact that he'd gotten his uncle out of trouble with those puffed-up secessionists for the moment wasn't going to keep him from coming up here looking for Austin as soon as they left the Big House.

He was still scoping out the furniture for a piece big enough for Bogie to crawl behind when he heard a low grumble. It wasn't coming from Bogie's throat—it was rumbling from outside.

Bogie stopped snuffling under the black walnut bureau and lifted his head, ears swinging. His forehead wrinkled, for all the world like Henry-James's did when he was concerned.

"It's just thunder," Austin whispered. "There must be a storm brewing."

The sky cracked and the rumbling rolled to a crashing peak. Bogie whined and looked wildly around.

"It's all right, boy!" Austin said. "It won't hurt you!"

But as a flash of lightning lit up the window, the dog dove for the bed and buried his face under the feather bolster. From beneath the covers there was another yelp, and Jefferson's dark head popped out.

"It's getting me!" he cried out. "Charlotte, help!"

Austin flew, spread eagled, onto the bed and clapped his hand over Jefferson's mouth.

"It's just Bogie, shrimp!" Austin hissed as he pulled the covers back over all three of them. "Hush up!"

Jefferson's sleep-puffy face was immediately a mass of dimples as he flung his chubby arms around Bogie's neck. Bogie rolled his eyes miserably and dug his nose under the little boy's undershirt. Jefferson giggled.

"Is he going to live with us now?" Jefferson whispered. "Now that Henry-James ran away?"

Austin grabbed on to Bogie as another clap of thunder rattled the window. "How did you know Henry-James ran away?"

"Charlotte told me. I was scared last night, so she slept in this room with me." He poked his head out from under the covers. "Where is she?"

"That's why you were calling to her," Austin said. "I thought you were dreaming. She must have gone back to her room."

"No, I didn't," a voice whispered from below them.

Austin scooted to the edge of the bed and hung over to look upside down. Charlotte was lying there on her belly, propped up by her elbows. She waved.

"What are you doing under there?" Austin said.

She pulled herself out and hiked up onto the high bed. "I hid when I heard you coming. I didn't know who would be with you."

"I told you Austin wouldn't run away," Jefferson said. He folded his arms importantly across his chest. "She thought you went off with Henry-James."

Charlotte shrugged inside her white nightgown. "Where *did* you go?"

"I fell asleep in the library. I didn't wake up until Uncle Drayton came in."

"Daddy's home?" Charlotte's freckles at once stood out.

Austin nodded. "Those men from Charleston stopped him on the road and made him come back. They were accusing him of letting Henry-James learn to read."

"He does know how to read," Jefferson said.

Austin stared at him. Charlotte's eyes bulged.

"He reads as good as me," Jefferson said. "'Cause I taught him."

"*You* taught him?" Austin said.

Suddenly, lightning forked outside the window, and a roll of thunder pounded down on the roof as if a herd of horses were racing across it. Jefferson screamed and yanked the covers over his head. Bogie wriggled down beside him, whining into the feather bed. Even Charlotte jumped and grabbed on to Austin's sleeve.

"That was a big one!" Austin whispered. He glanced at the window. The rain was coming down in sheets, slashing against the glass and shivering the panes. The room had grown evening-dark.

"I don't like these big storms," Charlotte said, eyeing the window. "We have them every spring."

The thunder crashed again, this time without its warning rumble. The wind hurled the sheets of rain into the side of the house, and Charlotte and Austin retreated under the covers with Bogie and Jefferson. Bogie panted and nuzzled his nose into Austin's armpit.

"Is this one of those storms that brings up the river?" Austin said.

"Yes," Charlotte said. "I've seen Rice Mill Pond get all the way up to the spring house."

"I've been wanting to see one of these—"

But with the next crack of thunder, Austin threw the covers back and sat straight up on the bed. Bogie whimpered and crawled halfway into his lap.

"Rice Mill Pond?" Austin said.

"Right. Why?" Charlotte said.

But as Austin's eyes went slowly to hers, she seemed to know.

"Henry-James," she whispered. "That pond will be over-flowing!"

Austin scrambled out of bed and threw open the wardrobe. A big pullover shirt, knee-high boots, and an old felt hat flew over his shoulder.

"What are you doing?" Charlotte asked.

"I have to go get him!" Austin said. "If the water gets high, he won't be able to walk from the island!"

"But neither one of us can swim either!" she said. "I don't know, Austin."

"I *do*," Austin said. And he did. There wasn't a question in his mind.

Charlotte watched him for a minute. Then she came off the bed and headed for the door.

"Don't go without me," she said, and she fled out into the hall.

Austin pulled the shirt over his head. When his head came through the hole, Jefferson was beside him, rummaging through the wardrobe.

"What do you think you're doing?" Austin said.

"Going with you. I can help find Henry-James."

"No!"

Jefferson jerked his head out of the wardrobe, and the look on his face jabbed at Austin like a kick in the stomach. There was no angry high-pitched scream, no hurling of shoes in a hissy fit across the room. There was only hurt in his tear-filled blue eyes.

"But I always go," Jefferson said. "I'm the one who taught him to read. He's my friend, too."

Austin helplessly shook his head. The thunder smashed across the sky again and the wind tossed another wall of rain against the glass. Bogie leaped off the bed and crawled underneath it. Austin squatted down in front of his little brother.

"I need you to do a job here," he said. "You have to keep Bogie hidden from Aunt Olivia. And you see how scared he is of the thunder—he can't go with us."

From under the bed, Bogie let out a pitiful whine.

Jefferson nodded, his blue eyes solemn. "Henry-James is gonna want him safe when he comes back, right?" he said.

Austin felt the lump in his throat. "Right," he said.

When he comes back, Austin thought as he slipped out the door with his felt hat pulled low over his face. And he remembered to add, *Jesus, please make sure he does come back.*

They got out the back door without being seen by anyone. Uncle Drayton and Aunt Olivia were talking in muffled voices in the drawing room, and everyone else seemed to be hunkering down from the storm.

And with good reason, Austin decided as he and Charlotte stepped out onto the back porch. If he'd thought the storm was loud from the inside, it was deafening outside. The wind alone made it impossible to hear even each other as they bent their faces down, grabbed on to each other's hand, and tore across the plantation toward the rice mill.

Already the water was seeping out of the grass and up over Austin's boot tops, but he couldn't hear his own footsteps for the howling of the wind and the beating of the rain. He did notice that there was no pounding in his head. He just seemed to know right where he was going.

They kept among the trees as they headed for the river. The Monarch Lakes had lost their butterfly shape and were oozing up onto the lawn to meet Rice Mill Pond. Austin and Charlotte splashed through the water, their clothes soaked and sticking to their bodies.

Austin could barely see the rice mill for the onslaught of rain, but he was sure he saw the dugout rise up off the top of the water and then drop with a splash.

"The river looks like the ocean!" Austin shouted to Charlotte.

She clenched his hand tighter.

She's scared, Austin thought. He clenched back. He was pretty scared himself.

"It's this way!" Charlotte cried, poking her hand out from under her green, soggy cape.

Austin blinked against the rain. The edge of the little pond nearest Rice Mill Pond had disappeared underwater, and Austin hardly recognized it. He had to lift his knees up almost to waist-level to run to it. Beside him, Charlotte lurched forward and nearly fell headfirst into the muck.

"I got tangled up in my cape!" she shouted.

Austin nodded and pulled her on. But when he got to the edge of the pond where they'd last said good-night to Henry-James, his heart plunged to his boot tops.

The island, too, had vanished under the water.

"Henry-James!" he shouted. "Henry-James, where are you? It's Austin—and Lottie!"

There was no answer except the angry bellowing of the wind and the pumping of Austin's heart in his ears as he squinted through the rain.

"Henry-James!" he shouted again.

"Wait! I think I see something!"

Austin shoved his dripping hat back and followed where Charlotte was pointing. At first he saw nothing but gray rain slanting its way to the choppy water.

"There!" she cried. She plunged out calf-deep into the water and pointed again.

This time, Austin saw it, too. There was something blue-green, wrapped around a bush that was holding itself up bravely out of the pond.

"Is that my shirt?" Austin shouted.

"Yes—and it has Henry-James in it!"

A jagged vein of lightning ignited the sky. In its flicker, Austin saw the black boy's face, tight and terrified as he clung to the bush. The whites of his eyes flashed in fright.

"What are we going to do?" Charlotte screamed to Austin. Her hood had blown back and her hair was plastered to the sides of her head like fur on a wet cat. Water poured off the brim of Austin's hat, and he flung it aside as he peered across the pond. The wind whipped up in a fresh gust, and the bush Henry-James clung to rocked with it.

"Austin!" Charlotte cried. "We have to do something!"

I don't know what to do, Austin's head pounded at him.

And then he stopped. *Jesus, please,* he pounded back. *I know You sent me here. Please help.*

Suddenly, Austin heard a crack, and Charlotte's scream rose to hysteria.

"The bush broke, Austin!"

To Austin's horror, Henry-James was swallowed up by the pond. His hands splashed above him, and his head bobbed up, only to disappear again under the surface.

Panic choked at Austin's throat. He knew exactly what Henry-James was feeling—that helpless sinking and grabbing and fighting-not-to-drown until someone saves you.

Austin pulled himself up straight. "Lottie!" he shouted. "Help me get a branch—a big one!"

Charlotte turned and tried to run, but once again her cape, heavy with pond water and rain, twisted around her legs. She stumbled and splashed into the shallow edge of the pond.

Austin looked wildly around and snatched up the first piece of wood he saw, a thick branch that had been ripped from an oak. He stuck it out to Charlotte and towed her in. By now she was sobbing.

"He's going to drown, Austin! We can't let him drown!"

But Henry-James hadn't drowned yet. Austin could see his head bobbing above the surface and his hands clawing the air.

"Grab on to the stick!" Austin shouted to him. "I'll pull you in!"

Austin thrust the branch out as far as it would go. From behind him, Charlotte latched on to his arm.

"He can't reach it!" she shouted. "Austin, he can't get it!"

Austin put one foot into the pond and the water surged up and inside his boot and down his leg. Austin leaned out farther and thrust out the branch. Henry-James's white-rimmed eyes spotted it, but his head vanished under the water again.

"He'll drown!" Charlotte was sobbing over and over. "He's going to drown!"

"No!" Austin shouted at her. "Stop it, Lottie. We can save him."

Please, Jesus. Please save him.

Austin stretched his waterlogged foot farther into the pond and once more jammed the branch into the distance between himself and his friend. With a frenzied splashing, Henry-James groped for it, but in vain.

And then there was another huge splash, almost into the middle of the pond, as something brown and wet and furry landed like a cannonball in the water.

✞ ✞ ✞

Chapter Seventeen

"**B**ogie!" Austin shouted.

A mass of brown fur and ears struggled to the surface and swam, big head tilted out of the water, toward Henry-James. The boy's frantic splashing stopped, and Austin saw two arms burst through the surface and wrap themselves around the dog's neck.

"Come on, Bogie!" Austin called to him. "Come on, boy!"

Charlotte hung on to Austin's arm harder than ever as he held the stick out over the pond. Head straining to stay above the wild water, Bogie splashed toward shore with Henry-James hanging around his neck like a harness. The big paws paddled and toiled, and he moved, inch by painful inch, closer to the pond's edge.

Behind him, Charlotte was still screaming, "Austin, please don't let him drown!" But Austin felt a surge of hope as he held the branch steady.

"Just a little farther, Bogie, and you can grab the stick! Come on, boy!"

Lightning once more lit up the sky. Austin knew a crash of thunder wouldn't be far behind. He coaxed Bogie more urgently.

But as the roar rocked the air, Bogie kept on swimming. And at last, he clamped his mouth around the stick, and Austin began to pull.

"Don't let go," he cried. "You've got it!"

Bogie didn't need persuading. He kept his jaws clenched on the branch until a limp and trembling Henry-James was all the way on the shore.

Bogie didn't even stop to shake. He lowered his big head over Henry-James and licked his ear. Charlotte flung herself over her friend's back.

"Henry-James? Wake up," she sobbed. "Austin, is he dead?"

Austin put his face close to Henry-James's nose. Bogie slurped Austin's ear, too.

"I think he's breathing," Austin said. Fear clawed at his insides. "We have to get him to some help, Lottie."

"Can we carry him?"

"We've got to!" Austin rolled Henry over and put his hands under his shoulders. "You grab his feet!" he shouted to Charlotte.

She nodded and got her hands around Henry-James's ankles.

"Lift!" Austin shouted.

But Henry-James hardly budged from the mud. He was slippery from the water, and his drenched clothes added extra weight.

Bogie danced backward and bayed.

"We're trying, Bogie! He's heavier than I thought!" Austin said. "One more time, Lottie!"

Again they squeezed their faces and sucked in their breath and tried to lift. They lugged Henry-James a few inches, and then he sank back into the mud.

Charlotte's face crumpled. "We're not getting anywhere!"

"Maybe we can drag him!" Austin said. The rain was falling so hard over his face that he had to shake his head to see. He got hold of Henry-James's wrists and began to tug. He walked backward and Henry-James slid slowly along the ground—and then Austin's boot hit something and he staggered.

A pair of thin arms caught him.

"Good Lord in heaven!" The voice was strong and stern and full of fear—and it belonged to Ria.

"Is he all right, Austin?" another voice said. "Is he still alive?"

Kady brushed past Austin and leaned with Ria over Henry-James's motionless body.

"He breathin' still," Ria said. "Come on, you chilrun. Help us carry him now."

It was as if a hand had reached down from above and scooped them up. Ria instructed them all where to hold on to Henry-James, and the four of them lifted him from the ground and moved away from the pond.

"I can hardly see where we're going!" Kady shouted.

"Bogie will show us the way!" Austin shouted back. "Take us home, Bogie!" he called to him.

Bogie wagged his tail purposefully and took off through the trees.

Daddy Elias had a fire blazing in the fireplace by the time Ria got Henry-James stripped out of Austin's wet clothes and wrapped in a quilt in front of it. While Kady put on a pot for boneset tea and Ria made a poultice from flax seed for

Henry-James's chest, Daddy Elias knelt on his old brittle knees beside Henry-James with his eyes crinkled shut.

"Lordy," he said as he rocked back and forth, "You sees our boy here all wore out and sick with sufferin'. I know if'n You holds him in Your arms, he gonna be all right. He gonna open them eyes and say, 'Daddy 'Lias.' If'n You reach down Your hand to him, Jesus, he ain't gonna die."

Austin jerked back from the fire where he sat, wrapped in a quilt. Beside him, Bogie jumped up with a start, too.

"Die?" Austin said. "He isn't going to die, is he?"

"Might could," Ria said. Her voice was as stern as ever—except for the tremble Austin heard at its edges. "Scared half to death, for one thing. And chilled right down to his bones."

The lump in Austin's throat swelled until it hurt. "I didn't mean for all this to happen!" he said. His eyes burned. "I didn't, Ria. You have to believe me."

"It isn't your fault, Austin," Kady said. She set the cracked cup full of tea down on the hearth and came over to him. "This isn't your doing. It's my father's. He even had *me* thinking there was nothing I could do to change things."

"I hate him!" Austin cried. He pushed past Kady and Bogie and flung himself toward the window. Tears were stubbornly pushing their way onto his cheeks. He swiped at them furiously. "I'm never going to forgive him for this!"

No one said anything. Except Daddy Elias, who murmured, "Mmmm-mmmm."

In a moment, Austin felt the old man at his elbow.

"You gots to forgive Marse Drayton, Massa Austin," he said.

"I can't." Austin wiped at the tears again, but several dripped off his chin.

"But ain't that what Jesus done for you?" the old man said.

"I don't know."

"Sure you does. You had you a different look in your eye when you come in here today. You knew Jesus gonna help you 'fore you even went out after Henry-James. Ain't that right?"

Austin nodded. He didn't trust himself to talk.

"Jesus done forgave you for tryin' to do His work, and He showed you you don't gots to do it alone. Now you got to keep listenin' to Him, Massa Austin, you got to pay attention when He say you gots to forgive, just like He do."

Austin struggled against his angry tears. "Uncle Drayton is still going to sell Henry-James, and he's still going to punish Lottie, and he's still going to send us away, no matter whether I forgive him or not."

Daddy Elias shook his head. "You listened to Jesus before. You do that again, Massa Austin. You just forgive Marse Drayton."

"Austin," Kady said, "we really ought to get back to the Big House now. I told Aunt Sally if we weren't back in two hours to send Daddy out looking for us."

"I don't want to leave Henry-James!" Austin said.

"I can take care of him," Ria said sharply. "You done enough."

Austin felt stung. Daddy Elias put a gnarled hand on his shoulder. "You go on now, Massa Austin," he said. "Jesus got Henry-James. And He got you, too, if'n you'll allow it."

Austin gave the tears one more swipe. "I'll try," he said. "I'll try really hard."

Polly and Tot met them at the back door.

"Daddy's in the library," Polly whispered as she pulled

them inside. "I'll distract him while you get upstairs. He'll never know you were out."

But a door opened behind her, and Uncle Drayton's crisp, unmistakable footfalls tapped the wood floor.

"Good heavenly days, what is it *now?*" he said.

His voice didn't trumpet. It had the weary sound of a tired bugle.

"Sorry," Polly whispered to Austin. "I tried."

Uncle Drayton moved her firmly out of the way and looked down at the wet, bedraggled trio standing before him, hands clasped behind his back. Austin felt Charlotte begin to tremble. Kady stiffened like a starched shirt.

"You were rescuing the slave boy, weren't you?" Uncle Drayton said.

Austin suddenly felt as if he'd done this all before—stood before his angry uncle, mind racing for yet another lie to tell just to do what he thought was right. But this time, Austin couldn't do it. The only thing that would come out was the truth.

"Yes!" he said. "He's our friend! He would have drowned if we hadn't."

"And all because you disobeyed me and taught him how to read," Uncle Drayton said.

"But you were wrong!" Austin said.

Uncle Drayton give a deep sigh. "Perhaps I *was* somewhat hasty."

Austin stopped with his next protest on his lips. Uncle Drayton pulled his hands out from behind his back, and Austin saw that he was holding a dog-eared pamphlet.

"Jefferson Davis has brought some questions to my mind—not the least of which is whether to follow anyone's heart but my own."

It was a rare moment. Austin didn't know what to say.

And then he did know. "Actually, sir," he said carefully, "Daddy Elias says it's Jesus' heart we have to follow."

"You never stop, do you, Austin?" Kady murmured beside him.

"I hope you never do," Uncle Drayton said. "It's your questionin' and talkin' and carryin' on that keeps us from acting like sleepwalkers."

The handsome smile, the one they hadn't seen on Uncle Drayton's tanned face for weeks, crept back into his eyes. "I think I need to ask some forgiveness. Kady?"

Kady looked carefully at her father. "Does this mean I can visit with Aunt Sally again?"

"I don't think that's the way it works," Austin said, head cocked. "I think you have to forgive him no matter what."

"Be that as it may," Uncle Drayton said quickly, "you may resume your talks with your aunt, Kadydid. But remember that you are still my daughter. As long as you are living under my roof, I must ask you not to turn anything you learn against me."

Kady tossed her damp curls. "Fair enough," she said.

Uncle Drayton turned to Charlotte. "Sweet thing?" he said softly.

She studied her soggy high-topped shoes for a moment. But the honey-brown eyes she finally lifted to her father were steady and sure. "It would be easier if I knew what was going to happen to Henry-James now."

"What's done is done," Uncle Drayton said. "As for whether any reading lessons continue—" For a moment, his golden eyes looked bewildered.

Austin felt himself holding his breath.

"As for that," Uncle Drayton said finally, "I must give that some serious thought."

Austin was still untangling that in his head when Uncle Drayton turned to him.

"I have said some harsh things to you, Austin. I confess I've blamed you for most of this."

Austin nodded woodenly.

"Will you forgive me, son?"

Austin's head pounded—but just a little. Daddy Elias's words seemed to erase the noise in his head. *"You got to pay attention when He say you gots to forgive—just like He done."*

Austin took a deep breath. It was something he'd said he could never do, but now he couldn't do anything else.

"I forgive you," Austin said.

Uncle Drayton closed his eyes as he nodded. "What can I do to make this up to you?" he said.

Austin shrugged. "You don't have to fix it . . . unless Jesus tells you you ought to do something."

Uncle Drayton's eyes softened. "You seem to have the Lord's ear. What do *you* think He might have me do?"

"Henry-James might die," Austin said. "From being locked up all that time and then staying out on that island and then almost drowning."

"Ria is doing her best out there in the cabin," Kady said, "but it's damp and they need more blankets."

"I'll send Isaac out with them right now," Uncle Drayton said. "Miss Pumpkin Polly—" Polly jolted to attention at the banister. "Go and tell your mother to gather five or six."

Polly exchanged glances with Tot, and Austin knew what

she was thinking. *Mama is going to throw a fit.*

"I think all of you had best get out of those wet clothes before you catch your death," Uncle Drayton said.

They started to scatter, but he put his hand on Austin's shoulder.

"Let me say one more thing," he said. "I lost two friendships this morning, and if I do what I've promised myself and stand up for my own beliefs about secession and educating my slaves, I may lose more than that." He shook his head sadly. "I only wish I had the kinds of friendships to take their places that you children have with each other. Did you know that our little man came down to me this morning and told me that he was the one who taught Henry-James to read?" He chuckled. "He offered to give up riding horses and eating Brown Betty forever if I wouldn't punish you."

"That makes up for him letting Bogie out," Austin said as the three of them dragged themselves upstairs.

"*I* let Bogie out," Kady said, "Ria and I. I saw you two from the window, heading out into the storm like you didn't have a lick of sense. I thought, 'Kady, you're so wrapped up in being mad, you can't even move. You are spineless as a snake compared to those two.' So I went looking for help and I found Ria."

"How did you know Bogie was in the house?" Austin asked.

Kady lowered her voice, eyes dancing merrily. "Mama was marching up and down the hall just a-sniffin' and saying, 'What is that horrid smell?' She was convinced it was something Polly had brewed to take away her freckles!"

"I bet Polly threw a fit," Charlotte said.

Kady stopped at her bedroom door and shook her head.

"No, she invited Mama in to search her room, so Ria and I could fetch Bogie and make our escape."

"Well, fancy that!" Charlotte said.

Austin felt a stab of guilt as he went to his own room. *I never would have believed that of Polly. I've been as bad to her as Uncle Drayton was to me. I had better ask her to forgive me.*

He stopped with his hand on his doorknob. An idea dawned in his head like an oil lamp flickering on.

That's how this forgiveness thing works! Uncle Drayton was wretched to everyone—especially Henry-James—but I forgave him. And I'm not half as good as Jesus. That's how He forgives me. No matter how bad I mess it up—or whether I can fix it or not.

And there wasn't a question in his mind about that.

Chapter Eighteen

When Austin woke up, the storm was over.

At least, the one outside. There was an even bigger one raging inside the Big House—just beyond his door.

"Drayton, I am absolutely appalled! The very idea of *slaves* using *our* things!"

"I know it's unusual, Olivia—"

"Unusual? It is absolutely dreadful! I only hope our neighbors don't get wind of this. It's bad enough that you're thinking about educating the darkies. Don't you realize what this will do to us? We won't be invited to a single party in town. Kady will be lucky to get a poor white for a husband—or do you plan to marry her to a Yankee, Drayton?"

Aunt Olivia appeared to be stopping for a breath. Austin was about to get out of bed and listen more carefully at the door when his aunt shrieked anew.

"Kady, what were you doing in *there?* Drayton, she was in Sally's room!"

180

"I know," Uncle Drayton said mildly. "I gave her permission."

"You did *what?* You did not discuss this with me!"

"It has nothing to do with you. I discussed it with Kady."

"Drayton, I am trying to make her fit to be a wife, not a—"

"Not a what, Mama?" Kady said. "A thinking, intelligent human being like Aunt Sally?"

Austin smiled to himself. The old Kady was back.

He thought about that as the voices volleyed back and forth in the hall.

Henry-James said that to me not long ago—that I was back. I guess having that angry stuff pounding in your head pushes the real you away somewhere.

Austin sighed. *But how do you keep from getting mad when there are so many awful things going on?*

"You gives them to Jesus," Daddy Elias would say. Austin cocked his head. And now he knew at least one way to do that.

Uncle Drayton and Aunt Olivia seemed to be taking their verbal battle down the stairs. Austin got up and peeked out into the empty hall and then padded barefoot to a door he'd never knocked on before.

"Who is it?" Polly said from inside.

"Boston Austin."

There was a stunned pause, and then Tot opened the door, lower lip hanging, black eyes big, and a bowl of something red in her hand.

"May I speak to Polly?" he said.

Tot moved aside, and Polly poked her head out from behind a mirror she had propped against her bedpost. Her cheeks were flaming red, as if she had a raging fever.

Austin looked into the bowl. "What are those?"

"Crushed camellia petals, if you must know. They're the last of them, and the roses haven't bloomed yet."

"You don't have to wait for the roses to bloom," Austin said. "It's the rose *leaves* that give your cheeks color when you rub them in."

"How would *you* know?" Polly said, and then she held up her hand. "Never mind. I know, you read it."

Austin nodded. "I also read that the mistake you made with the beet juice is that you probably didn't mix it with rose water. Although even plain beet juice is better than red iron oxide barn paint, which some women use—"

"Did you come in here to share beauty secrets?" Polly said as she went after her cheeks with a wet rag.

"No," Austin said. "I came to ask you to forgive me."

Polly stopped in midrub. "What?"

"I hope you'll forgive me for being so hateful to you and not believing that you really wanted to help. It was really ugly of me."

Polly blinked at him. Tot, of course, did the same.

"I don't guess you can help being so suspicious, being a Yankee and all," Polly said finally. "Aren't you people all like that?"

"I don't know," Austin said. "But I'm trying to change. I think that's what Jesus wants me to do."

Polly looked suddenly uncomfortable. She shrugged her narrow shoulders. "Well, I'm not going to tell anything you and Charlotte and Kady do, but don't get any ideas—it isn't because I'm lovey-dovey with all of you."

"Of course not," Austin said.

"It's because I don't want you to tell about what Tot did.

You know, last winter—"

"I told you I never would," Austin said. "No matter what."

"Even if I don't forgive you?"

"Right."

She looked into the mirror for a moment. "Well, I do," she said. "Now would you please leave us alone? Tot and I have things to do."

Austin shrugged and went out the door. From out in the hallway, he heard Polly say, "Where can we get some rose water, Tot?"

"Well! There you are!" said a soft voice behind him.

Austin whirled to see his mother standing like a fragile doll outside her door.

"Mother!" Austin said. "What are you doing up?"

"Feeling much better, now that I've gotten some things off my chest."

"Your cough?" Austin said as he joined her.

"No, some anger. I had a talk with your Uncle Drayton just a little while ago. I started off giving him a piece of my mind, and then he did the oddest thing."

"What?"

"He interrupted me right in the middle and asked me to forgive him."

"Did you?"

"Of course! How could I do anything else?" She put her hand on Austin's shoulder.

Austin stood still. "Mother, while everybody's forgiving everybody, do you think you could forgive me for something?"

She looked at Austin with her eyebrows gently lifted. "Whatever for, Austin? I was the one who told you to go ahead and teach Henry-James how to read."

"It's not about that. It's about that letter—the one I never wrote to Father."

"Ah," she said. Her eyes looked a little disappointed, but she tucked one of Austin's hands between her thin ones. "Why didn't you?"

"I didn't want to go. I still don't."

"Well, neither do I, now," she said. "If Uncle Drayton is indeed asking himself serious questions, and he's going to stand up for keeping the South in the Union and some other things he talked to me about, he's going to need my support—yours, too."

"So you forgive me?"

"What you did—or didn't do—was wrong," she said.

Austin looked at the floor, but she cupped his chin with her hand.

"But I would forgive you no matter how it turned out, Austin. If I didn't, there would be so much anger between us, and nothing turns out right when people are separated by anger."

As if someone had given her a cue, Ria rushed up the stairs. As soon as she saw Austin, her eyes hardened. Austin looked helplessly at his mother.

"How is our boy?" Mother said.

"He doin' fine, Miss Sally," she said, still eyeing Austin grimly. "He'll stay that way, if'n he can keep hisself out of trouble."

"Ria?" Austin said. "Will you forgive me?"

She grew so stiff that Austin thought she might break in half before his eyes.

"Please?" Austin said.

Ria managed a sniff. "For one thing I can," she said. "I

forgives you for settin' Henry-James free from that shed. I was fixin' to do it my own self, but Bogie come runnin out at me and near to ripped my clothes off. Now I knows it was you chilrun put him up to it."

Austin's mouth was going dry. "But you won't forgive me for teaching Henry-James to read."

Ria didn't move. "That was Henry-James's choice," she said. "What my heart be hard 'bout is—and 'scuse me for sayin'—it's 'bout the ideas you put in my boy's head, things he ain't never thought about till you come here talkin' 'bout readin' and freedom and all like that."

"But those aren't bad ideas!" Austin said.

"Maybe not for you," she said. "But if'n he keeps them things in his head, I'm gonna lose my boy sure as you and me be standin' here, Massa Austin. My heart ain't gonna forgive for that."

She looked as if she wanted to walk away, but she stood still and drilled her eyes into the floor.

"Ria," Mother said, "please go back and tend to your son. I don't need your help today."

"Yes'm," Ria said. "But I'll get you settled back to your room first."

She turned her back to Austin and took Mother by the arm.

Austin hurried to his own room, pulled on his clothes, and took off toward Slave Street. When he opened the door to the cabin, a weak voice greeted him.

"What's the matter with you, boy?" Henry-James was propped up against a pile of blankets and pillows in lacy cases.

Austin couldn't resist a chuckle.

"You laughin' at me?" Henry-James said, scowling.

Austin shook his head and sat happily next to him on a pallet.

"You're better," he said.

"I is. Now all I wants to know is when I gets to get up."

"You don't like this?" Austin said.

"Sure I likes it," Henry-James said. "I'm just 'fraid I'm gonna get used to it, is all, 'fore I have to go back to slavin'."

Austin glanced anxiously at the door. "Henry-James?" he said. "Were you better off before I put ideas about being free and all into your head?"

Henry-James pulled his face into a scowl again. "You think I ain't never had an idea of my own, Massa Austin? You wasn't the one told me I wanted to get free. You just tol' me how I'm gonna do it."

Austin blew air out of his mouth and made his deer-colored hair dance on his forehead. "Do you know you're about the only person here I didn't have to ask forgiveness from?"

"Not Miss Lottie?"

"Oh, no, not her either."

"Or Bogie?"

At that, there was a bumping of bones under the table, and Bogie emerged, eyes bloodshot from so many interrupted naps.

"Hey, boy!" Austin said. He felt his face break into a grin as he hugged the dog's loose, furry neck.

"You gonna keep an eye on him till I gets up?" Henry-James said.

"We'll all take care of him—Charlotte and Jefferson and me. Don't worry about a thing."

Henry-James closed his eyes. "I always worry when you's involved, Massa Austin," he said drowsily. "Don't nobody never know what you's gonna come up with next."

By midafternoon, the sun came out, and Charlotte, Jefferson, Austin, and Bogie sloshed across the lawn to their place on the river. The slaves were back in the rice fields, moving across them in a row as they hoed.

"That's a good thing," Charlotte said as the children climbed up to a low branch to watch and Bogie settled himself on a patch of high ground below. "That means the seed had already took hold and the rain didn't wash it away."

It's a good thing for Uncle Drayton, Austin thought. *But it's a bad thing for the slaves. They have to work so hard.*

That was still confusing—Uncle Drayton turning out to be a good man after all, yet still owning other human beings. But at least there were other things that made sense in his mind . . . and in his heart.

Jefferson, it seemed, felt the same way.

"Uncle Drayton isn't going to punish me for teaching Henry-James to read," he said, swinging his legs cheerfully.

"That's good," Charlotte said. She grinned over his head at Austin, and her freckles seemed to dance.

"And he's going to take me riding tomorrow," Jefferson went on. "And Polly called me a brat today." He gave a contented nod. "I think everything is going to be all right."

Austin grunted. "We all want you to be happy, shrimp," he said. "Because when you're not, nobody else is happy either."

"Now that's not really true," Charlotte said, tipping her head thoughtfully. "He hasn't pitched a hissy fit in a long time."

"But I might throw one soon," Jefferson said.

Austin rolled his eyes. "Why?"

"If we don't play the Jesus game right quick. Did you all forget about Jesus?"

Austin gave his head a firm shake. "Nope," he said. "Never. Let's play us a game of Jesus right now."

Jefferson giggled. "Bogie can be the donkey! What can Maximillian do?"

Austin had no idea what Maximillian could do as he swung down from the tree. But he did know Jesus was right there with them.

And there was no question in his mind about that.